TO MOM, DAD AND ALEX. – E.G.

BIG PICTURE PRESS

First published in the UK in 2024 by Big Picture Press,
an imprint of Bonnier Books UK,
4th Floor, Victoria House
Bloomsbury Square, London WC1B 4DA
Owned by Bonnier Books
Sveavägen 56, Stockholm, Sweden
www.bonnierbooks.co.uk

Design copyright © 2024 by Big Picture Press
Illustration copyright © 2024 by Evangeline Gallagher
Text copyright © 2024 Adam Roberts

1 3 5 7 9 10 8 6 4 2

All rights reserved

ISBN 978-1-80078-675-2

This book was typeset in Stallman Round and URW Geometric.
The illustrations were created in pen and ink.

Edited by Charlie Wilson
Designed by Olivia Cook
Production Controller Ché Creasey

Printed in China

TALES FROM BEYOND THE STARS

ADAM ROBERTS
EVANGELINE GALLAGHER

BPP

8
ABOUT
THIS BOOK

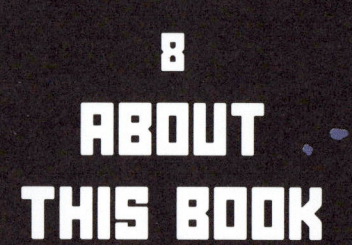

10
THE STAR
BY H G WELLS

20
THE FATHER OF
SCIENCE FICTION

56
FROM THE EARTH
TO THE MOON
BY JULES VERNE

76
THE WAR OF
THE WORLDS
BY H G WELLS

74
A JOURNEY INTO
THE UNKNOWN

94
INVADERS FROM
OUTER SPACE

22
MICROMÉGAS
BY VOLTAIRE

38
THE AGE
OF DISCOVERY

40
THE LAST MAN
BY MARY SHELLEY

54
PLOTTING
THE PLAGUE

96
HERLAND
BY CHARLOTTE PERKINS GILMAN

108
WRITING
THE FUTURE

110
BUCK ROGERS:
ARMAGEDDON 2419 AD
BY PHILIP FRANCIS NOWLAN

124
FROM PAGE
TO SCREEN

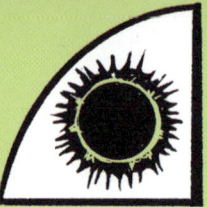

ABOUT THIS BOOK

There are various histories of science fiction as a genre, and various theories as to when it started. For some, the first science fiction dates back to ancient Greece, with stories of people flying to the Moon in sailing boats caught up in gigantic storms. For others, science fiction is bound up with modernity, industrialisation and developments of technology. Some say that it dates from 1927, when American author and editor Hugo Gernsback coined the term. But most people peg the origins of the genre to the nineteenth century, emerging alongside the technological advances and social upheaval of the Industrial Revolution. According to author Brian Aldiss, Mary Shelley's *Frankenstein* (1818) is the first true science fiction novel: a monster story in which the monster is created by science, not magic; a Gothic tale in which technology and its consequences haunt the world. Aldiss considers this one of the core science fiction stories: a fable of how unintended and terrible consequences can follow technological invention, howsoever optimistically intended. His thumbnail phrase for this: 'Hubris clobbered by nemesis'. Shelley also rewrote the apocalypse, taking the end of the world out of religious myth and placing it in terms of scientific explanation: a plague that wipes out humanity in *The Last Man* (1826).

If science fiction started with Shelley, it came to proper fruition later in the nineteenth century. In France, Jules Verne sent characters on extraordinary voyages (the *voyage extraordinaire*

is another core science fiction story): into a hollow earth in *Journey to the Centre of the Earth* (1864), into space and around the Moon in *From the Earth to the Moon* (1865), and round the entire solar system in *Off on a Comet Servadac* (1877). Verne was also the inventor of gigantic machines and technological marvels around which he based stories: *Twenty Thousand Leagues Under the Sea* (1870) imagines a gigantic, electrically powered submarine decades before such craft were actualised, *The Steam House* (1880) includes a gigantic robot elephant, and *Robur the Conqueror* (1886) a vast flying warship, again powered by electricity.

British author H G Wells reimagined the extraordinary voyage. In *The Time Machine* (1895), his protagonist travels not in space but in time, to a far-future world in which humanity has devolved into two species: the fey, childlike Eloi who live above ground, and the troll-like Morlocks, who emerge from their subterranean dwellings at night to devour them. Wells published a series of science fiction novels in the 1890s that created whole sub-genres: *The Island of Doctor Moreau* (1896), about 'uplifted' animals altered by science to approach humanity; *The Invisible Man* (1897); *The War of the Worlds* (1898), the first alien-invasion tale; and *When the Sleeper Wakes* (1899), the first dystopia.

By the beginning of the twentieth century, the genre was set to explode. In France, Georges Méliès' adaptation of Verne's *From the Earth to the Moon* became the first science fiction movie. Pulp magazines, printed on cheap wood-pulp paper and with brightly coloured coal-tar-dye cover art, proliferated through the 1910s and 1920s. By the 1930s, science fiction had entered its golden age.

THE STAR

It was on the first day of the new year of 1900 that the announcement was made that the motion of the planet Neptune, the outermost of all the planets in our solar system, had become erratic. The eminent astronomer Ogilvy, at the Hastings observatory, had already called attention to a 'suspected change in its velocity' in December – but phrasing it in this way was hardly calculated to interest the world. In truth, mostly people were blissfully unaware of the existence of the planet Neptune.

But the discovery of a remote speck of light in the region around Neptune had caused some excitement among scientific people, who had found the intelligence remarkable enough, even before it became known that the new body was rapidly growing larger and brighter. The motion of this body alone was quite different from the orderly progress of the planets.

The fact was that a massive object had come rushing without warning into the radiance of the neighbourhood of the Sun – and it was causing quite a stir.

One day after the announcement, it was clearly visible to any decent instrument, a speck with a sensible diameter, in the constellation Leo. On the third day of the new year, the newspaper readers of two hemispheres were made aware for the first time of the real importance of this unusual apparition in the heavens. 'Planetary Collision Imminent!' was the headline in one London paper, and the eminent French astronomer Duchaine was quoted as saying that the new planet would probably collide with Neptune.

At dawn on the sixth of January, early risers in London were just starting their day when they saw something shocking. A yawning policeman saw it, people in the busy crowds at the markets stood agape, workmen setting out to work, the drivers of news-carts, labourers trudging afield, poachers slinking home all saw it – a great white star, appearing suddenly in the westward sky. It was brighter than any star in our skies, more brilliant than the evening star at its brightest. It glowed out white and large, no mere twinkling spot of light, but a small, round, clear, shining disc, just an hour after the day had come.

In a hundred observatories there was a suppressed excitement, and a hurrying to and fro, to gather photographic apparatus and spectroscopes. For it transpired that Neptune had been struck, squarely, by the strange planet from outer space and the heat of the concussion had instantly turned two solid globes into one vast mass of incandescence. It was a gigantic world, a sister planet of our Earth.

Two hours before the dawn, the pallid great white star shot around Earth, fading only as it sank westward, and the Sun mounted above it. And when next it rose over Europe, crowds gathered on hilly slopes, on house-roofs, in open spaces, staring eastward for the rising of the great new star. It rose with a white glow in front of it, like the glare of a white fire, and those who had seen it come into existence the night before cried out at the sight of it.

"It is larger," cried the people clustering in the streets. "It is brighter!" But in the dim observatories the watchers held their breath and peered at one another. "It is nearer," they said.

The next night the star rose later, for its proper eastward motion had carried it some way across Leo towards Virgo, and its brightness was so great that the sky became a luminous blue as it rose, and every other star was hidden in its turn, save only Jupiter near the zenith. It was very white and beautiful. The world was as brightly lit as if it were midsummer moonlight. One could see to read quite ordinary print by that cold clear light, and in the cities the lamps burnt yellow and wan.

Everywhere the world was awake that night, and a sombre murmur hung in the air over the countryside like the belling of bees in the heather. Soon, this murmurous tumult grew to a clangour in the cities. Before long, the tolling of the bells in a million belfry towers and steeples summoned the people to sleep no more and to gather in their churches and to pray.

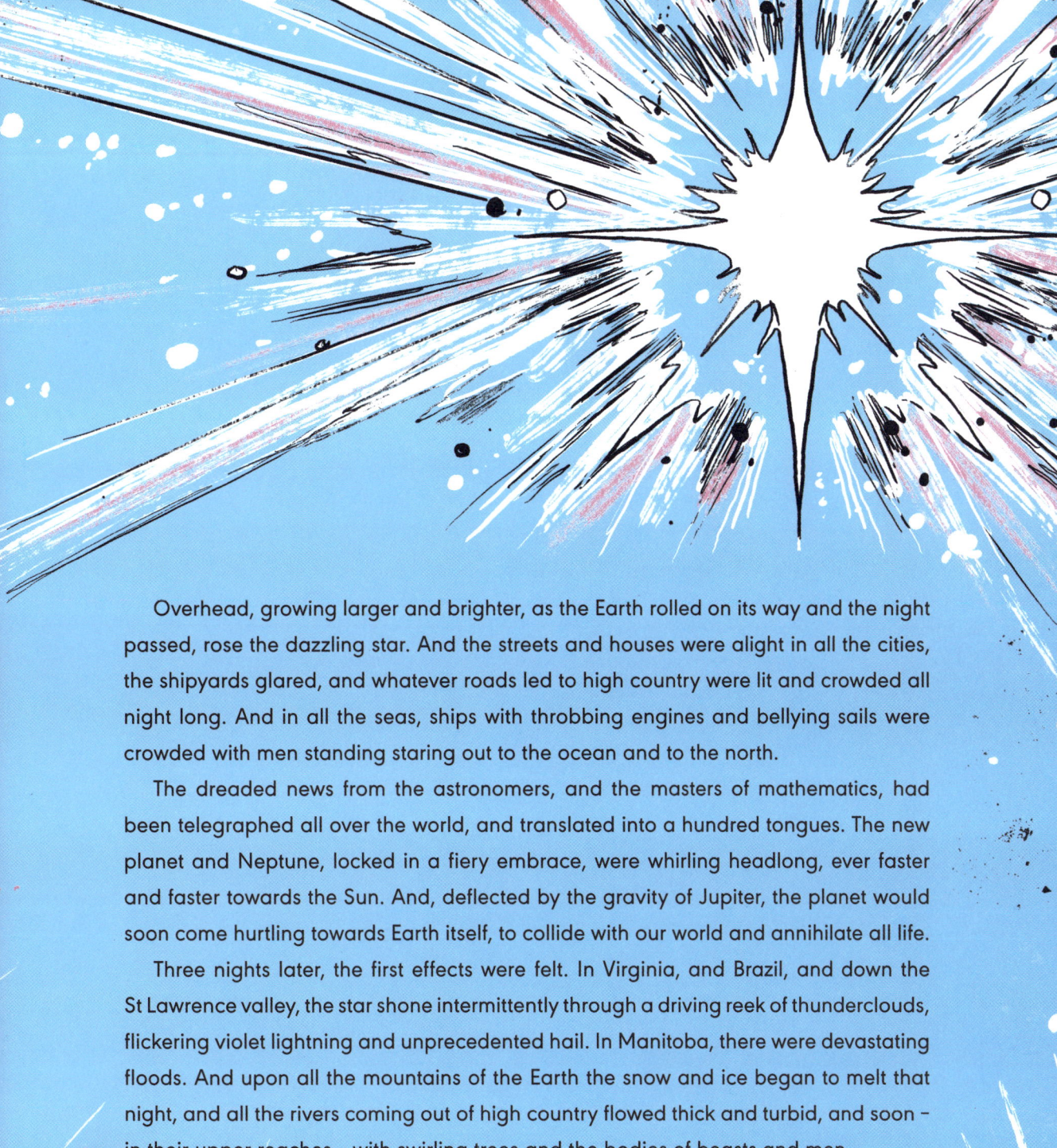

Overhead, growing larger and brighter, as the Earth rolled on its way and the night passed, rose the dazzling star. And the streets and houses were alight in all the cities, the shipyards glared, and whatever roads led to high country were lit and crowded all night long. And in all the seas, ships with throbbing engines and bellying sails were crowded with men standing staring out to the ocean and to the north.

The dreaded news from the astronomers, and the masters of mathematics, had been telegraphed all over the world, and translated into a hundred tongues. The new planet and Neptune, locked in a fiery embrace, were whirling headlong, ever faster and faster towards the Sun. And, deflected by the gravity of Jupiter, the planet would soon come hurtling towards Earth itself, to collide with our world and annihilate all life.

Three nights later, the first effects were felt. In Virginia, and Brazil, and down the St Lawrence valley, the star shone intermittently through a driving reek of thunderclouds, flickering violet lightning and unprecedented hail. In Manitoba, there were devastating floods. And upon all the mountains of the Earth the snow and ice began to melt that night, and all the rivers coming out of high country flowed thick and turbid, and soon – in their upper reaches – with swirling trees and the bodies of beasts and men.

That night, the heat grew so intense that the rising of the Sun was like the coming of a shadow. The earthquakes began and grew until all down America from the Arctic Circle to Cape Horn, hillsides were sliding, fissures were opening, and houses and walls were crumbling to destruction. The whole side of Cotopaxi slipped out in one vast convulsion, and a tumult of lava poured out so high and broad and swift and liquid that in one day it reached the sea.

So the star continued its march across the Pacific, trailing behind it thunderstorms like the hem of a robe. A growing tidal wave toiled behind it, frothing and eager, pouring over islands and sweeping them clear of people. Until that wave came at last – in a blinding light and with the breath of a furnace, swift and terrible it came – a wall of water, fifty feet high, roaring hungrily, upon the long coasts of Asia, and swept inland across the plains of China.

For just a moment, the star showed with pitiless brilliance the wide and populous country; towns and villages with their pagodas and trees, roads, wide cultivated fields, millions of sleepless people staring in helpless terror at the incandescent sky; and then, low and growing, came the murmur of the flood. China was lit with a glowing white, but over Japan and Java and all the islands of Eastern Asia, the great star appeared as a ball of dull red fire because of the steam and smoke and ashes the volcanoes were spouting forth to salute its coming.

Larger grew the star, and hotter, and brighter, with a terrible swiftness now. The tropical ocean had lost its phosphorescence, and whirling steam rose in ghostly wreaths from the black waves that plunged incessantly, speckled with storm-tossed ships.

The next day, the star did not rise. In a moment of reflection, the inhabitants of Earth set their eyes upon the old constellations they had counted lost to them forever. In England it was hot and clear overhead, though the ground quivered perpetually, but in the tropics, the constellations Sirius and Capella and Aldebaran showed through a veil of steam. When at last the great star rose near ten hours late, the Sun rose close upon it, and in the centre of its white heart was a disc of black.

Those looking up, near blinded, at the star, saw that a black disc was creeping across the light. It was the Moon, coming between the star and Earth. And even as people cried at this respite, out of the East with a strange inexplicable swiftness sprang the Sun. And then star, Sun and Moon appeared together across the heavens.

There were still people who could perceive the meaning of these signs. The star and Earth had been at their nearest point, had miraculously swung about one another, and the star had passed. Already it was receding, swifter and swifter, in the last stage of its headlong journey downward into the Sun.

And then the clouds gathered, blotting out the sky, and thunder and lightning wove a garment round the world. All over Earth was such a downpour of rain as had never before been seen, and where the volcanoes flared red against the cloud canopy there descended torrents of mud.

The inhabitants of Earth braced themselves for what was to come. For weeks the water streamed off the land, sweeping away soil and trees and houses in the way, and piling huge dykes and scooping out titanic gullies over the countryside. Those were many days of darkness that followed the star. All through them, and for many weeks and months, the earthquakes continued.

But as time went on, the inhabitants of Earth, hunger-driven and gathering their courage slowly, crept back to their ruined cities, buried granaries and sodden fields. Ships that had escaped the storms of that time were brought back to once familiar ports. And as the storms eventually subsided, it was noted that the days were hotter than of yore, and the Sun larger, and the Moon – shrunk to a third of its former size – took now fourscore days between its new and new.

Earth was changed irrevocably. This story cannot delve into the depths of these changes – it concerns itself only with the coming and the passing of the star. But changes there were. The inhabitants of Earth found that a strange change had come over formerly snowbound Iceland and Greenland and the shores of Baffin's Bay, such that the sailors coming there presently found them green and gracious and could scarce believe their eyes.

The Martian astronomers – for there are astronomers on Mars, although they are very different beings from men – were naturally profoundly interested by these things. They saw them from their own standpoint, of course.

'Considering the mass and temperature of the missile that was flung through our solar system into the Sun,' one wrote, 'it is astonishing what little damage Earth, which it missed so narrowly, has sustained. All the familiar continental markings and the masses of the seas remain intact, and indeed the only difference seems to be a shrinkage of the white discolouration (supposed to be frozen water) round either pole.' Which only shows how small the vastest of human catastrophes may seem, at a distance of a few million miles.

THE FATHER OF SCIENCE FICTION

Though he wasn't the first person to write in the genre, H G Wells (1866–1946) is known as 'the father of science fiction' for a reason. In part this is because he innovated so many varieties of the form, writing works of enduring influence. *The Time Machine* (1895) was the first story about a 'traveller' using technology to move through time; *The Island of Doctor Moreau* (1896) was the first story about 'uplifted' or medically adapted animals acquiring a kind of humanity; *The Invisible Man* (1897), though not the first story about invisibility as such, is the first to premise invisibility on scientific, or pseudo-scientific, grounds. Wells was an endlessly restless innovator, publishing multiple books and many short stories every year of his long writing life. In *The First Men in the Moon* (1901), a scientist builds a spaceship out of an anti-gravity material and effects a lunar landing, finding a hive-like alien species living there. *Anticipations* (1901), a non-fiction book, projects then-current technologies into the future, making a series of predictions, many of which came true. Indeed, Wells developed quite the reputation as a kind of prophet. *The War in the Air* (1908) speculated about the development of nuclear weapons long before they were actually invented, and how they would change the nature of war: it was Wells who coined

the term 'atom bomb'. His short story 'The Land Ironclads' (*The Strand Magazine*, 1903) was the main inspiration for the British government putting money into research and development of the tank as a weapon of war. When he saw actual tanks in action on the battlefield, Wells wrote, 'They were my grandchildren – I felt a little like King Lear when first I read about them.' (*War and the Future*, 1917)

But there's another sense in which it's right to consider Wells the father of science fiction: he was skilled at capturing 'sensawunda', science fiction fans' term for the excitement and wonder invoked by the grandeur and vision of science fiction. Fantasy works by a sense of enchantment, and science fiction by a sense of wonder. In the eighteenth century, this quality was called 'the sublime', a sense of vastness, majestic scale, cosmic enormousness, the infinitude of the universe and of our smallness compared to it. There is a thrill in this. The disparity in scale might evoke in us awe at infinite splendour, or might generate terror at the overwhelmingness of it all. Back in the 1650s, French scientist Blaise Pascal, examining the cosmos using the then-new technology of the telescope, understood just how large everything is. He said, 'The eternal silence of these infinite spaces terrifies me.' This sense of human precariousness in the face of cosmic vastness, the indifference of the universe, is at the heart of a great deal of science fiction. Wells' 'The Star' is one of the earliest great articulations of this theme.

MICROMÉGAS

On one of the planets orbiting the star Sirius lived a young man, whom I had the honour of meeting during the course of a voyage he made to our little anthill.

He was called Micromégas: a fitting name, for he was both micro – small – and mega – huge. Small because he developed a fascination for microscopy, and the science of miniature things; but large because he was, by our human standards, huge indeed. He stood, in his stockinged feet, some twenty-five miles high.

A great height! But when you consider that our Milky Way galaxy is fifteen million miles wide, and that there are billions of such galaxies in the universe, you can see why he called himself micro. But to a human being, he was a towering giant, who lived among others of his kind. His world is vastly larger than ours, just as Sirius, the brightest star in our sky, is much, much larger too. The truth is, towards the centre of the galaxy, everything is bigger: stars, planets, life-forms. The further out one travels, towards the rim and edge of the galaxy, the more attenuated everything grows: thinner and smaller. Such is cosmic providence.

As a youth – for the first 250 years of his life – Micromégas lived a conventional existence. He went to school and studied well. Like all his kind, his bones were made of a material stronger than titanium, and his muscles were proportionately vast to be able to lift and move his colossal limbs. The gravity of his home world was a dozen times as strong as Earth's. The Sirians organise their society around a religion that worships the barycentrum, the great blaze of a million close-packed stars at the centre of the galaxy. According to the holy scriptures of Sirius, this is the dwelling place of

God and her angels – beings a million miles tall, a millionfold more intelligent, and capable of pure creation and pure appreciation. The Muftiya of this world teach that out of this location God has laid down the law and judges her followers for obeying or disobeying.

All scientific enquiry is directed towards the centre of the galaxy: giant telescopes and receiving instruments that capture and analyse all the radiation that pours from this super-dense and super-hot place, sifting it for religious messages or revelations. The galactic core was too hostile an environment to travel to, but it could be studied, watched, examined.

But from an early age Micromégas found his interest oriented in a different direction. He studied telescopy, as all well-born Sirian youths do, but instead of building even bigger observatories to peer in greater detail at the galactic core, he reasoned that the same technology of lenses and focal tubes could be turned around and used to examine the very near rather than the very far. It had never occurred to any Sirian to invent a 'microscope', or to peer into the realms of the minuscule, for as the Muftiya taught, only the mega mattered, and the galactic core above all. But Micromégas constructed just such a device and began to make notes of the microscopic life he could see.

23

At the age of 400, when he first attended Sirian university, Micromégas published a book of his discoveries, illustrating the text with his own hand. He had not only observed but managed to dissect some of the smallest insects that inhabited the Sirian home world – flies and spiders no larger than 100 feet long in some cases – and by increasing the magnification he saw into an even more minute world than that. Microbes barely a yard across, pulsing protozoa or blobs of cellular matter six feet wide, their membranes shimmering with wriggling tentacles, their bodies translucent in the white Sirian sunlight. He was even able to discern viruses that were barely a foot wide, like globular folds of tripe.

The publication of this book, however, made many people angry. The chief Muftiya of Micromégas's home country declared that it was a heretical work, the result of a wilful individual who had, quite deliberately, turned away from God and busied himself with nonsense of a dangerous, sacrilegious kind. Then the police arrested Micromégas's publisher and confiscated all copies of the work. Micromégas himself was outraged: "I am pursuing science!" he declared. "All that we see, everything in this cosmos, is made by God, the very small just as much as the very large. It is not heretical, and is in fact holy and good to explore and admire this creation on every scale."

The matter went to court. The prosecution argued that God had made the microscopic too small to see for a reason: to hide it from observation. The proper religious focus was on the very large, and most especially the galactic core, which could be studied through religiously sanctioned telescopes. Micromégas retorted that he was using the same technology as telescopes but reassigned. "We would not know all the things we do know about the galactic core without telescopes," he told the court. "Does that mean that God did not want us to know these things? Of course not. A telescope is a tool, and so is a microscope. Through it the fullest range of God's splendour is revealed."

The court was not persuaded by his argument. Micromégas was sanctioned, fined, expelled from university and commanded to stop his irreligious microscopic studies. In disgust, he left not only his home country but his home world.

The Sirians, having an average IQ of 8,000, had long ago mastered space flight. Rockets, powered by concentrated electrical discharge, rose from their planet and scudded around their solar system. But the primal stellar fires of so many stars concentrated at the galactic core prevented them from venturing in that direction, and no other direction held any appeal to them.

After his sentence was handed down, Micromégas retreated to his family estate in the Sirian highlands. He spent a year assembling a ship and working on the electrogalvanic motors that would lift it into the sky. He stowed enough supplies for a hundred years: food and drink, but also air, for the aether of the spaces between the stars is too rarefied for breathing. Finally he bade farewell to his mother and father, took his seat at the prow of his craft and steered it from a clifftop in his parents' estate and into the air. He floated like a sesame seed, gliding in a slow ascent until he was able to engage the motive shaft and rise himself into the empyrean expanses of space.

For three years Micromégas steered his craft from star to star, each time moving further from the centre of the galaxy and towards the scattered and diminished rim. Finally he arrived in our solar system, intrigued by the variety of planetoids that orbited our Sun: some were mere baubles, like Jupiter and Saturn; others were mere specks.

His first port of call was Saturn, where he skimmed over the technicolour rings. His ship was so large, by our standards, that even the inhabitants of Saturn – a planet some nine times as large as Earth, and home to a race of beings no more than 6,000 feet tall – noticed it.

An emissary from that world was sent up in a Saturnian balloon, and Micromégas, eager to make friends, invited this individual aboard his craft. When he first stepped aboard, Micromégas could not help but burst into laughter: to him such a dwarfish figure – barely a mile high! – could not but seem comical. But at once he stopped himself and apologised. "Forgive me my bad manners, sir," he told his visitor. "I am not used to seeing individuals of such diminished height."

The Saturnian bowed and introduced himself: "I am the Grand Secretary of the Academy of Saturnian science."

"Micromégas of Sirius, at your service, sir."

"What might I do to please you, sir?" asked the Secretary.

"I do not wish to be pleased," answered the voyager. "I wish to be taught. Tell me about your world. How many senses do the inhabitants of your planet possess?"

"We only have seventy-two," said the Saturnian, "and we always complain about it. Our imagination surpasses our needs. We find that with our seventy-two senses, our rings, our five moons, we are too restricted; and in spite of all our curiosity and the fairly large number of passions that result from our seventy-two senses, we have plenty of time to get bored."

"I well believe it," said Micromégas, "for on our planet we have almost 1,000 senses, and yet we are still only too conscious of our limitations. For we know that in the galactic centre there exist much more perfect beings, whose capacity to process sense-data, and whose powers of intellect and emotion, approach infinity. How long do your people live?"

"Oh! For a very short time," replied the small man from Saturn. "Most of us are lucky to last 500 revolutions around our Sun. This is a matter of intense regret to us."

"It is the same with us," said Micromégas. "How we complain about it! It must be a universal law of nature. We feel we die almost at the moment we are born; our existence is a point, our lifespan an instant, our planet an atom. I would fear burdening you by telling you that our lifespan is 700 times longer than yours. It seems to me all the more reason to fill such time as we do have with useful and productive work.

I, for one, am on a voyage of discovery into the lesser reaches of the galaxy."

"Does our splendid solar system constitute one of these lesser places?" asked the Saturnian, growing almost offended at the way Micromégas was talking.

"I mean nothing insulting when I say so," the Sirian replied. "It is a simple matter of size. The people on my world worship the very big, and entirely ignore the microscopic. But I am different. I have travelled in this direction, to where the stars and planets, and indeed the inhabitants, such as yourself, good sir, are miniaturised. It fascinates me."

"Then, dear sir," said the Saturnian, "I would advise you to visit the third planet from our Sun. Its inhabitants call it Earth."

Micromégas at once called up Earth on his devices, peering through his advanced telescope. "But that is a mere atom!" he exclaimed. "Barely a clod, spinning through space. Do you tell me it is inhabited?"

"Indeed, sir," said the Saturnian. "And by a large number of very busy individuals."

"Then let us depart at once, and investigate," said Micromégas. "I am more curious than I can say."

The Saturnian was happy to remain upon Micromégas' giant craft, which again engaged its electrical motile power and swept through the empyrean as a gull soars on an updraft. The Sirian steered over the north pole of Saturn and set his space-rudder to guide the craft towards Earth.

Arriving at Earth, Micromégas was at first amazed at the barrenness of the place.

"See," he told the dwarf from Saturn, "how poorly constructed this planet is! It is so irregular and has such a ridiculous shape! Everything here seems to be in chaos: you see these little rivulets, none of which run in a straight line, these pools of water that are neither round, nor square, nor oval, nor regular by any measure; all these little pointy specks scattered across the surface?"

"The inhabitants call those mountains," the Saturnian returned. "And though everything appears irregular to you here, you say so because everything on your home world is drawn in straight lines. But I assure you not only is this a genuine world, but a populous one."

This was the most extraordinary thing Micromégas had ever seen. He had studied, by means of his own microscopes, the smallest creatures, single-cellular beings, bacteria and animalcules upon Sirius. But none of them had been sentient or possessed of intelligence.

He soon saw it was as the Saturnian said: upon the world were millions of these bacteria, and yet every one was a thinking, feeling creature. Each, indeed, considered what they thought and felt – especially what they felt – to be the most important thing in the universe. If Micromégas had laughed a little at the sight of the Saturnian dwarf, he positively howled with laughter at the presumption he discovered amongst these folk.

He spent several months observing the inhabitants through one of his small microscopes (a mere 2,000 feet in diameter). From one of the oceans he was able to pluck up a tiny fish – what we on Earth call a blue whale – and to hold it before his eye, before returning it again. Seeing a different species of whale in the Baltic Sea he picked this up too, only to discover it was a sailing ship, and swarming with miniature crew.

It was at this point I first made the acquaintance of the mighty Micromégas. For I was ship's doctor upon this very vessel. The ship was returning from the Arctic Circle, where it had made a number of scientific observations. It was reported in the news that our vessel was caught up by a gigantic hurricane and whirled through the sky, but the truth is the vast finger and thumb of the visitor from Sirius picked us up.

Micromégas skilfully seized our vessel, putting it on his fingernail without pressing it too hard for fear of crushing it.

The others aboard, terrified by this development, rushed below decks to hide, but my scientific curiosity was greater than my fear. I stood on the poop deck and called to the face – so large it seemed to reach from horizon to horizon – asking who it was, and what it intended to do here.

Of course, he could not hear me! To his huge ears, my voice was tinier than the most minute buzzing of a gnat. But, bringing up one of his microscopes, he examined us, and so could see that I was on deck, gesticulating and moving my mouth.

"It is extraordinary," he said to the dwarf from Saturn. "There is a creature here barely as big as an atom, and yet shaped like you or I – taking the form of an intelligent being. Might the inhabitants of this tiny world be intelligent?"

"We can hardly find out without speaking with them," the Saturnian replied.

And so Micromégas set our ship upon a metallic plate within his ship and situated a powerful microscope above. To us, aboard the boat, it seemed that the sky had changed colour and bizarre new moons loomed hugely above us – the light with which Micromégas illuminated his microscopic plate was whiter and brighter than the Sun had ever been, and the structure of the scope itself, from our perspective, looked like a smooth, clear moon. From time to time, great clouds, nebulas in the new sky, drifted back and forth – Micromégas and his Saturnian companion walking about.

But Micromégas was at work. He constructed a new kind of device out of the horny substance from which fingernails are made, and which is called in Greek *keras*, shaping this with infinite delicacy. Tubes captured our voices and magnified them so that Micromégas could hear – at the same time taking his vast and booming tones and shrinking and elevating them to render them intelligible to us. He called this device, as he afterwards informed me, the keratone.

It was for him a simple matter to learn our language, his intellect being so massively greater than ours.

The other members of the ship's crew, becoming habituated to our new circumstances, came out from below decks. But none of them were prepared to converse with Micromégas, since the ship's parson told them that his was certainly the voice of the devil. And so it fell to me to talk.

Micromégas said to me, "I see more than ever that one must not judge anything by its apparent size. God! You who have given intelligence to substance that is so immensely small! But to you, this is as worthy a soul as that possessed by beings immensely large."

I replied, "It is indeed strange to encounter beings so much larger than we humans. But I have always held that intelligence is not limited to size. A tall man may be a fool, a short one a genius. Our great Roman poet Virgil says that bees – insects greatly smaller than we – think and communicate."

Micromégas said, "You intelligent atoms, in which the Eternal Being desired to make manifest his skill and his power! Surely you taste pure joys on your planet; for having so little matter, and appearing to be entirely spirit, you must live out your life thinking and loving, the veritable life of the mind."

At this, I had to be truthful. "Some of us, perhaps, live in such a way. But this is not the way for most of humanity. I must be honest, my friend: a great many human beings are mad, vicious and wretched people, only too ready to do evil, if evil comes their way." At this point I considered the war between Christian Russia and Muslim Turkey that was, at that point, being fought – it lasted, as you will know from your history books, from 1735 to 1739 – and said to our visitor, "Did you know that, as I am speaking with you, there are a hundred thousand madmen of our species who like to wear hats, killing a hundred thousand other members of our species who prefer to wear turbans, or else being killed by them? The truth is this is how we have used almost the entire surface of the Earth since time immemorial."

"But why?" Micromégas asked in a pained voice.

"For a piece of dirt considerably smaller than your little toe," I said. "The possession thereof."

At this, Micromégas grew indignant. "But this is too cruel! Who could conceive of such an excess of maniacal rage! It makes me want to lift up my foot and crush this whole anthill of ridiculous assassins."

I will confess I was alarmed at this, but I kept my cool. "There is no need," I said. "We are working towards such a conclusion on our own, I assure you."

At this, he calmed himself. "I am bitter," he told me, and informed me of his story – how he hoped, by travelling away from the true giants of the galactic centre, worshipped by his people, towards the miniaturised outskirts of the Milky Way, he would disprove the ethos of his people, which believes size equals virtue and smallness evil. "Sadly, it seems it is the case that these intelligent atoms are dedicated to violence and war!"

At this I was eager to reassure him. "It is true that our species is only too addicted to war, but not all of us dedicate our lives to this savage practice. We have amongst us people devoted instead to the pursuits of peace: to art and culture, to scientific enquiry and the realm of pure thought."

This heartened Micromégas. "Where might I find such people?"

I told him: the Paris Academy of Arts and Science. It was an easy matter for him, then, to pick up our entire ship with tweezers and deposit it in the Tuileries Garden in the very heart of the city! You can imagine the astonishment with which the citizens of Paris regarded the appearance of an entire ocean-sailing ship, complete with its crew, on dry land so many hundreds of leagues from the sea!

I hurried into the Academy and made the learned men and women inside acquainted with the existence of Micromégas, and his much smaller, though still colossal, companion.

At first, I was misbelieved, but as the various scientists and philosophers came out to take a look at our ship, it was a simple matter for Micromégas to address them, through his keratone.

"Since you are amongst the number of wise men and women inhabiting this tiny world," he told them, "and since apparently you do not kill anyone for money, tell me, I beg of you, what occupies your time."

"We dissect flies," said one philosopher. "We measure lines, we gather figures; we agree with each other on two or three points that we do not understand."

It pleased the Sirian and the Saturnian, then, to question these thinking atoms, to learn what it was they agreed on. For hours the discussion ranged from physics to chemistry to biology, and so on to questions of metaphysics and religion.

"Your knowledge is at a very elementary state," Micromégas said. 'But do not worry. I speak with the greatest kindness."

He promised to make them a beautiful philosophical book, written very small for their usage, and said that in this book they would see through to the final end, the point of everything. And indeed, he gave the world this book before he and the Saturnian took their leave and flew away through the infinite spaces of the galaxy. It was taken into the library of the Paris Academy and put on display. Anyone can consult it there. I myself went the other day and sat in the library and turned the pages of this book, from start to finish.

It is nothing but blank pages.

THE AGE OF DISCOVERY

One difference between science fiction and fantasy is that the latter creates worlds that operate by means of magic, where science fiction is inspired by actual scientific knowledge. How this is done varies. 'Hard' science fiction adheres closely to the actual laws of nature: stories extrapolate, but do not violate, actual scientific possibility. 'Soft' science fiction might bend those scientific rules, although it will generally stay within the realm of what is not too implausible. For example, in real life it is not possible to travel faster than light. Even with the fastest possible spaceship, travelling the immense distances between the stars would take decades or centuries. A 'hard' science fiction writer will respect this fact; a 'soft' might evade it, utilising faster-than-light technology like a warp drive.

Stepping back a couple of centuries, we can see a different expression of the disparity of scale between the universe and our human existence. In *Micromégas*, the great French author who wrote under the name Voltaire (his actual name was François-Marie Arouet; 1694–1778) created a story of space exploration: part witty satire on the small-mindedness of eighteenth-century French science, part exploration of the wonder of our vast and marvellous universe. Micromégas himself is a twenty-five-mile-high giant from a planet circling the star Sirius, who flies around the galaxy by

harnessing the power of electromagnetism – and sometimes by riding comets – and examines all he finds with scientific passion. Upon arriving in our solar system, he meets a Saturnian who is, by comparison, a dwarf, being only a mile high. Together they travel to Earth, whose inhabitants – us – appear to them like ants.

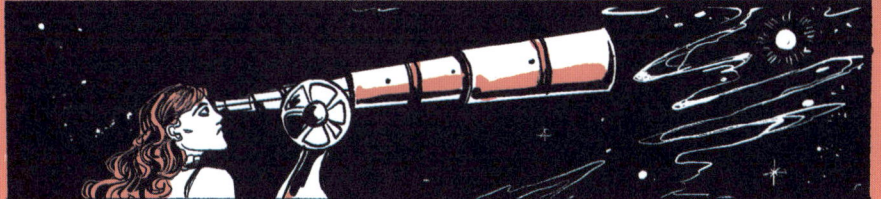

The Saturnian 'dwarf' is a caricature of Bernard Le Bovier de Fontenelle (1657–1757), perpetual secretary of the *Académie des Sciences* in Paris. Voltaire at the time had ambitions in that direction, which Fontenelle thwarted. Upon reading Voltaire's *Eléments de la philosophie de Newton* (1738), he said, 'Very good, Monsieur Voltaire. Another three years of study and perhaps you will actually begin to understand Newton.' Voltaire was fond of satire. His *Candide* (1759) brilliantly lampoons German philosopher Gottfried Leibniz (1646–1716). The book's characters suffer indignity, mutilation, assault and starvation, and witness untold horrors, all the time repeating Liebniz's 'All is for the best in this, the best of all possible worlds.'

But *Micromégas* is not all satire. Though the story makes fun of Fontenelle, it is also full of marvels and wonders. Though the mile-high 'dwarf' Saturnian is a figure of fun, Micromégas himself is not. He is Isaac Newton, a figure whom Voltaire greatly admired (he called him 'our Christopher Columbus' and 'the scientific god to whom I sacrifice'). Newton was the first to calculate accurately the distance of the star Sirius, hence Voltaire's choice of that star. Newton is *micro-* because he was physically small (as a child, his mother used to say he was tiny enough to fit inside a quart pot), but also *-megas*, huge, because he was a giant of science.

THE LAST MAN

I was visiting Naples in the year 1818. On the eighth of December of that year, my companion and I crossed the bay, to visit the antiquities which are scattered on the shores of Baiæ. I shall never forget that day: a bright winter Sun shone upon the translucent blue waters, revealing beneath the waves the ruins of old Roman villas, interlaced by seaweed, receiving tints of white and mother of pearl from the chequering of the sunbeams. On the far shore we entered the cave of the Sybil. In ancient times, the priestess of Apollo dwelled there, issuing prophecies. It was said that the god gave her glimpses of the future, and that the pressure of these visions disordered her wits, meaning that her prophecies were often riddles and her warnings misunderstood.

What we found inside was a chamber filled with these old prophecies: written upon parchment and bark and even upon clay tablets, in a variety of languages: Latin, ancient Greek, ancient Chaldean, Egyptian hieroglyphics. But one scroll I picked from the heap bore upon its outside – to my amazement – an inscription in modern English. How can this be? I asked myself, astonished. There has not been a Sybil in this place for thousands of years!

I was of course curious as to what this scroll contained, and so took it away with me when we left the cave. And here, I have written out the text. In some places the text was broken off or corrupt and I have restored its meaning.

My name is Lionel Verney. I am the last man alive upon the whole world. I can do anything at all, for there is nobody to stop me, and there is nothing I can do, for there is nobody to care.

In brief, my life: I grew up in an aristocratic family in the very heart of the green fields and dark forests of England. My father was a personal friend of the king himself, and we were often at court. But alas, my father – a dear man, kind-hearted and clever – had a problem; say rather a sickness, a disease. He was a gambler, and when gaming took possession of him he became fevered and unreachable. He lost everything. At first, the king cast him away as a friend – His Majesty could no longer associate with so notorious a gambler. We were reduced to penury and my father, in his shame and despair, took his own life.

Then, in 2073, the king died. The public mood had changed with respect to the monarchy, and a referendum was held that signalled the end of the monarchy in our country. The Prince of Wales – Adrian, who was once my childhood friend – gave up all claims to the throne and was reduced to Earl of Windsor. It was there that, by chance, we met again – he out hunting one day, me gathering berries from the hedgerows and bushes to provide a meal for my sister Perdita and myself. He recognised me, despite the fact that he had last seen me as a child and I was now fully grown. "I could never mistake you, Lionel," he cried, leaping from his horse and embracing me. "You and Perdita cannot be left to dwell in a rude cottage. Come!" And so Perdita and I came to live with Adrian at Windsor Castle, which was now his home.

It was a tonic to my intellect to be able to spend hours in his library, reading every book. My sister and Adrian spent much time together, and there was another visitor – Lord Raymond. This ambitious young nobleman was the darling of the hour. He had recently returned from the continent, where he had been conducting military efforts on behalf of the freedom of Greece, against the oppression and invasion of the Turks. Lord Raymond had raised a battalion and fought nobly and well. But he had returned to his native land a wounded man – not wounded physically. Indeed, he nursed a different kind of injury: in his soul.

With him came a beautiful young Greek, Evadne Zaimi: a princess in her homeland. I fell instantly in love with this young woman. She was intelligent and full of passion. But alas, or alas for me, though she befriended me, and though we shared many tender conversations, her heart was already disposed. She loved Lord Raymond.

Raymond was aware of this, and it underlay his easy familiarity with me. We would often practise shooting together in the castle grounds and discuss literature and politics. "You support Adrian's abdication?" I asked him one day.

"As the Latin phrase has it, *vox populi vox dei*," said Lord Raymond, easily. "The voice of the people is the voice of God. And the people wanted the monarchy to end."

"You believe, then, in democracy?"

"I believe," he said, "that the people should be allowed to vote for their leader – the Lord Protector of the realm. And that once that leader is elected, he should be allowed to do whatever he chooses!"

It was then that I understood why Raymond had returned to England: the wound in his soul was ambition. He hoped to win the upcoming election, and to become the most powerful person in the country! "What of Evadne?" I asked.

"I care for her," he replied, offhandedly. "And her poor country, afflicted by Turkish invasion. But there are more important concerns."

I suspected that he was thinking not of Greece, but of his own country and his political ambitions. Would the people of England vote for him if he married a Grecian? My suspicions were confirmed when I saw Lord Raymond begin to woo my sister.

I am ashamed to say that, for myself, I dared to hope this might make Evadne receptive to my suit, and another marriage would follow. But it was not to be.

For a month the castle was caught up in the campaign for the election. Lord Raymond toured the whole country, giving speeches and making grand promises, and Perdita went with him. I was not surprised when the election returned Lord Raymond as Lord Protector.

Shortly after election day Evadne came to see me. "Now that Raymond is Lord Protector," she told me, "I see that his attentions will all be on this country, with nothing for Greece. I must return there and wished to say goodbye before I left."

I begged her to stay. But I could see her love for her homeland was greater than her love for me. And so she went.

For the first week of his new administration, Lord Raymond did not even notice that Evadne was gone. He moved to London and took up the many duties – and powers – of command. Adrian congratulated him on his success, but confided to me that he considered the Protectorship a poisoned chalice – a burden. "I fear that Raymond will not find it as glittering a prize as his ambition led him to believe it to be," he said.

And so it proved. For although Lord Raymond rejoiced in the trappings and splendour of high office, the business of governance wearied and depressed him. I would visit my sister in their official London residence and find her grey with worry. "He is a changed man," she told me. "Each day brings new stresses. Famine in the north – disaffection amongst the people in the west – and now plague."

This was the first I had heard of the coming disaster.

Plague! This enemy to the human race had begun early in June to raise its serpent-head on the shores of the Nile; parts of Asia, not usually subject to this evil, were infected. It was not like any of the previous sicknesses that have afflicted humankind. The sufferer would be hale and well one moment, and then an instant later would be doubled over coughing. His skin would taint, with green and yellow streaks spreading from the chest across the torso and down the legs. Rheum would pour from the eyes and slime from the nose. Some died within the day, shivering and moaning in their beds. Others lasted a few days. But all died eventually.

The sickness was reported to have reached Constantinople with many casualties, but I am ashamed to say we, in colder climes, ignored this as simply part of the way of things during the summer of the torrid zone. How wrong we were!

I was in my rooms one morning, at Windsor castle, when Raymond burst in. "Where is Evadne?" he demanded. "What have you done with her?"

"She has returned to Greece, to join her countrymen and countrywomen's fight against the Turks!" I exclaimed.

Raymond flung himself upon my chaise longue. "Then she has abandoned me!"

"Come now," I remonstrated. "You are Lord Protector! You are married to my sister! You have hardly been abandoned."

But it seemed, for all his declarations otherwise, that Raymond had more in his heart for Evadne than he had admitted – to others, perhaps even to himself. That day he stormed out, furious. And the next day I read in the newspapers that he was personally to lead a British military intervention in Greece.

At this I became truly worried. I took the next electric locomotive into London and rushed round to see my sister. "Think of the dangers of the region," I told her. "War – but also plague. You must dissuade him."

But neither plague nor war could prevent Perdita from following her husband or induce her to utter one objection to the plans which he proposed. And though Raymond was married to my sister, he had become obsessed with Evadne. When she had been with him, he had ignored her; now she was gone, he craved her.

I accompanied the British expedition, telling myself that I could at least try, being there, to keep my sister safe. We took the balloon service from London to Rome, and then another dirigible from Rome to Thessalonica. Raymond was greeted with cheering crowds wherever he went. He spent a week mustering an army before marching it eastwards to join the battle at the Greek-Turkish borders.

I went with him, but as his memoirist, not as a soldier. I promised him I would write the account of his life. "Be sure, Lionel," he instructed me, "to tell the truth. I do not care for flattery, or eulogies. Tell the world that I came because my heart was here!"

I believed it was! But not in the sense that the people took his words to mean.

I shall not weary this narrative with accounts of the fighting. Most of the battles were desultory affairs, for the Turkish army was already falling apart: under-strength due to the plague. The victorious Greeks, led by Raymond, marched on Constantinople.

On the outskirts of this mighty city, in amongst the lemon trees and upon copper-coloured soil, we marched slowly, for the landscape was littered with the corpses of those who had fought before, many wearing the uniforms of the Greek army.

Suddenly I heard a piercing shriek. A form seemed to rise from the earth; it flew swiftly towards me, sinking to the ground again as it drew near. I dismounted and discovered, amongst the banks of dead bodies, none other than Evadne! She was grievously wounded, dying. I held her in my arms and pressed my water bottle to her lips. Finally she gasped. "This is the end of love!" she cried, as if a prophetic fury were on her. "I die and – O my Raymond, there is no safety for thee!"

Raymond came, but too late. When he arrived, she was dead. We buried her in a marble tomb overlooking the Hellespont, and embraced one another in our mutual grief. The dazzling Sun and glare of daylight deprived the scene of solemnity.

"I shall march on Constantinople!" Raymond declared. "I shall free it in her name!"

The order was sent out through the army to proceed immediately towards the city. But the plague was already spreading through our troops: we left men too sick beside the road, some in tents, others lying on the bare ground under trees or bushes, to provide some small shelter from the relentless Sun. Many died where they fell.

It was unutterably shocking. I wept, in part to see fellow human beings suffering and dying, and in part from fear – for it preyed on my mind that I might catch this sickness and die as these pour souls were dying.

Soon enough we reached Constantinople, and Raymond ordered trenches dug and advances made. Raymond's eyes were fixed on the city. "One month," said he. "One month at the most, and she will fall to us."

At first the inhabitants of the city put up some resistance: shots were fired from the battlements, and occasionally a cannon blasted an explosive shell into our camp. But after a few days, all was silence. Rumour spread through the camp that everyone inside Constantinople had died of the plague – and that it would be suicide to enter the place. Desertions from our troops increased, our army melting away.

Finally, Raymond acted. "I will ride into the city myself, alone," he declared, before a muster of the whole army. "When I return to you, it will be as the victor of Byzantium!"

He sent sappers to set explosives against the main gates, and when they were blasted to shivers he mounted his horse and rode forward into the city.

He did not ride out. Hours passed, and the army grew restless. Eventually, and despite the danger of plague, I myself went into the city, on foot. Beyond the walls was a charnel house: corpses littered every street, dead bodies everywhere. I checked each in turn, but none were Raymond.

I found him eventually. The Turks had set a trap and he had ridden into it – an explosive mine, set behind a wall, triggered by his passage, that had crushed him.

The following weeks are a blur to my memory. Poor Perdita was distraught with loss at Raymond's passing, an empty shell, save for her grief. She did not utter a word.

I could not lay Raymond to rest in that cursed city Constantinople, and so I used what authority I still had to take a ship and sail it down the coast and across the blue Aegean Sea to Athens. But the city he had beloved was empty – its graveyards overfull, its charnel houses crammed with corpses, every house dark and filled with dead. The plague had reached the city before me.

Here I erected a tomb with my own hands, processing my grief for Raymond as much as for Evadne.

It was the year 2092, but calendars meant nothing to me. I do not know why the plague did not kill me, as it had killed so many others. I had been often exposed to its pestilence, and yet had not so much as sickened. And yet everywhere people died. For many weeks I was prostrated with grief: I wept for the strangers I saw, dead everywhere, and wept to think of the people I knew and loved, dead far away.

During the journey from Athens, my dear sister Perdita succumbed to her grief and left this mortal plane for what I hoped was peace beyond.

In time, the intensity of my sorrow dulled, and I grew homesick. I left, as the Bible says, the dead to bury the dead. I took a small skiff, crossed to the heel of Italy, and then sailed along the coast to Marseilles. Everywhere I passed was marked by death. Where people still lived, they shunned me – for perhaps I carried the pestilence with me, and they did not wish to be exposed. The network of balloon-boats that had linked the world in rapid travel was at an end: I saw not a one in all my voyaging. There was nothing for it but to walk the length of France, eating what I could along the way, drinking from the fresh streams.

At Calais there were people, and some who were prepared to welcome me. I slept in a bed in an inn, and on the morrow bought passage on a boat across the channel. The pilot was a talkative fellow, seemingly delighted at the news of the chaos the plague had spread. "It rages, sir," he told me. "Ships arrived in Ireland carrying survivors from America, but they were a lawless population, and set themselves to plundering Ireland and Scotland. Then they tried invading England! King Adrian – though he refuses the title – was our saviour. He raised an army against them and defeated them. The people would gladly crown him, but he refuses the royal name, and so is in all but electoral recognition the Lord Protector."

I did not tell this man of my friendship with Adrian. And before the ship docked at Dover, he died, poor fellow. He must have been sick with the plague, though he had shown no symptoms before we set out. Of course it came on him suddenly, as this disease always did. When the crew found him in his cabin, his skin lurid with green-yellow streaks, moaning and weeping, they panicked, took the ship's longboat and rowed away, leaving me and a handful of other poor passengers stranded at sea.

I had lost all fear of the pestilence: if it killed me, good. If not, I needed not live in terror of it. But I could not sail the ship single-handed. When it drifted in sight of the white cliffs of Dover I leaped overboard and swam the remainder of the journey.

The land to which I returned, alone, wet, was sadly changed. I had a store of gold sovereigns in my belt, but they were of no use. The usual patterns of commerce and exchange had broken down. Everywhere were pyres burning dead bodies, and strangers with scarfs around their mouths and wild eyes, warding me away. I walked to London, eating what I could – stale bread from an abandoned bakery, fruit and nuts, milk from cows in the fields abandoned by their farmers whose udders were swollen and painful.

London was filled with wild dogs, and was otherwise bare of people. I took my leave and walked west, along the Thames to Windsor, which I knew so well.

Here, astonishingly, I met some remnant of civilisation. Adrian was in residence, and his personal guard manned the perimeter of the castle. By preventing any sick person from entering they had preserved themselves. I could hardly believe it: my friend, still alive! Again I wept, but tears of joy. It took some persuading for the guards to take a message to my old friend, but I got through and was received within. Adrian had aged, or been aged by events, to a shocking degree. "My dear Lionel," he exclaimed. "It is indeed good to see you." I rushed to him and embraced him.

I informed Adrian about Lord Raymond's unfortunate passing and the loss of both Evadne and Perdita, which still hung heavy on me despite the long and arduous journey I had endured and the suffering I had witnessed during my travels. How so much loss could be endured, I did not know.

While Adrian was aware of the tragic event, he had not been told all the distressing details of Raymond's death during the siege of Constantinople, which I chose to spare him. In this way, he could remember our friend as he was, rather than thinking of the tattered remains that had been left behind following the bloody battle, the memory of which still haunted my waking thoughts.

Life in Windsor and the surrounding land was, because of the loyalty Adrian himself commanded, as close to the old normality as anywhere I had seen. People tilled the fields, treated one another with respect, worked and lived. But one morning a black sun arose – an orb the size of our regular Sun, but dark, whose beams were shadows, ascending from the west as the Sun arose in the east. In an hour it reached the meridian and eclipsed the bright parent of day. Night fell upon every country, night, sudden, rayless, entire. The stars came out, shedding their ineffectual glimmerings on the light-widowed Earth. The shadows of things assumed strange and ghastly silhouettes. The wild animals in the woods took fright at the unknown shapes figured on the ground. They fled. Birds, strong-winged eagles, suddenly blinded, fell in the marketplaces, while owls and bats showed themselves welcoming the early night. The citizens were filled with greater dread.

"It is a dire omen," Adrian declared. "A sign that this land will become uninhabited soon. We must depart!"

His plan was to take his people away from England and into France, where the weather was more congenial, and hope of a plague-free existence beckoned. It was no use to tell him that I had recently travelled though France and found it more plague-struck than anywhere. He would not hear it.

We gathered possessions and a great procession left Windsor, pulling hand-carts, riding horses, traipsing on foot.

I will not draw out this narrative of despair much longer. The plague was already amongst us. Many died before we got to Dover, and more before we landed in France. We found a vacant land, corpse-strewn, barren. Such people as we encountered had fallen under the spell of a dark preacher, a man who spoke ragingly of preparing our souls for the end of the world. Adrian led his people as far south as Switzerland, but here, our band reduced to a few dozen exhausted souls, we stopped.

"We must press on," Adrian insisted. He found a boat moored at a jetty in Lake Geneva and, when nobody would accompany him, set out in it. But, alas, a storm blew up and we stood, crying aloud, as the little craft broke and sank, drowning Adrian, Earl of Windsor and the last Lord Protector of England.

I do not know why I was spared the plague. But such was my malign fate. I watched every single person around me sicken and die.

Finally, fearing that I was the last human left on Earth, I followed the path along the Apennine Mountains, walking all the way to Rome.

And this is where I now am. In all my thousand leagues of walking, I encountered nobody, nothing but empty cities, no person except unburied corpses. My only companion is a dog, a shaggy fellow, a sheepdog whom I found chasing sheep in the Campagna. His master was dead, but nevertheless he continued fulfilling his duties in expectation of his return. His delight was excessive when he saw me. He sprung up to my knees; he capered round and round, wagging his tail, with the short, quick bark of pleasure: he left his fold to follow me, and from that day has never neglected to watch by and attend on me, showing boisterous gratitude whenever I caressed or talked to him.

His pattering steps and mine alone were heard when we entered the magnificent extent of nave and aisle of St Peter's. We ascended the myriad steps together, when on the summit I turned to gaze on the country.

I am, I am convinced, the last man left alive. Shall I wander the beauteous shores and sunny promontories of the blue Mediterranean? Strike out further, to Syria and Asia Minor (I would avoid Constantinople, the sight of whose well-known towers and inlets belonged to another state of existence from my present one) – perhaps walk as far as China, or explore the Russian steppes? There is none to prevent me, and equally none to applaud. Perhaps in some place I touch at, I may find what I seek – a companion. But I fear not. The plague has taken the whole of humanity, only I alone excepted.

Well: I shall go. I have chosen my boat and laid in my scant stores. I have selected a few books; the principals are Homer and Shakespeare. I form no expectation of alteration for the better; but the monotonous present is intolerable to me. Neither hope nor joy are my pilots – restless despair and fierce desire of change lead me on. Thus around the shores of deserted Earth, while the Sun is high and the Moon waxes or wanes, the planets will behold the tiny bark, freighted with Lionel Verney – the LAST MAN.

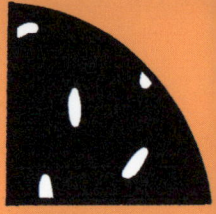

PLOTTING THE PLAGUE

Mary Shelley's *Frankenstein* (1818) is, as noted in the introduction, taken by many as the first proper science fiction novel. Its story of the Swiss scientist, Victor Frankenstein, who creates a living being – not by stitching together dead body parts, as in the movie adaptations, but by some mysterious process the book refuses to impart – is extremely famous. Attempting to create a beautiful humanoid, Frankenstein inadvertently creates a being of hideous ugliness. Horrified by what he has done, he runs off, leaving this creature to fend for itself. Shunned and attacked by all who encounter it, it grows hostile to humankind, taking revenge upon its creator's family.

This very famous story needs no summary here. Instead, this volume contains her later novel, *The Last Man* (1826), a tale of a world-ending plague. Shelley was married to Romantic poet Percy Bysshe Shelley, and was friends with Lord Byron and other famous Romantic writers. *The Last Man* is, in part, a fictionalised version of her friendship group, what is called a *roman-à-clef*. Adrian is based on Percy Shelley and Raymond is Byron, with Lionel being a gender-swapped version of Mary Shelley herself. But more remarkable is the novel's futuristic world, and the powerful account of the way plague devastates it.

Disease has been a constant of human existence ever since there have been humans. A plague is a disease that comes into a community from somewhere else. Sometimes, as with the Black Death in fourteenth-century Europe, or the nineteenth-century introduction of smallpox and typhus into Native American populations by Western colonists, plagues can effect devastating reductions in population numbers. But after a while, immunity develops amongst survivors. Shelley imagines a plague against which there is no immunity.

At this time, imagined futures were a new thing. The first book ever set in the future had appeared only a few decades earlier: Louis-Sébastien Mercier's *The Year 2440* (1771). Some writers used the new form to imagine utopian futures, in which revolution led to a peaceful and tolerant world, as in Constantin Volney's *The Ruins of Empire* (1791). But some writers looked into the future and saw disaster. Lord Byron's long poem 'Darkness' (1816) imagines a secular end of the world when the Sun, inexplicably, goes out. Humankind struggles in the lightless cold, society collapses, crops cannot grow and eventually mankind dies out. In French writer Jean-Baptiste Cousin de Grainville's *Le Dernier Homme* ('The Last Man', 1805) humanity becomes sterile and infertile, and so the population dwindles away. Mary Shelley took her title, but nothing else, from de Grainville's book. Hers is the first secular plague novel. It stands at the head of a rich tradition (these words are being written a few months after the Covid pandemic struck the whole world): plague fiction. Edgar Allan Poe's 'The Masque of the Red Death' (1842), M P Shiel's *The Purple Cloud* (1901), Jack London's *The Scarlet Plague* (1915), Michael Crichton's *The Andromeda Strain* (1969) and Stephen King's *The Stand* (1978) all owe something to it.

FROM THE EARTH TO THE MOON

The cannon was so big it couldn't be mounted. It had to be dug into the earth. It was the biggest cannon ever constructed by human beings, powerful enough to shoot a capsule so fast it would achieve escape velocity, leave Earth and travel all the way to the Moon.

"I stand by my belief that it will never work," declared Captain Nicholl of Philadelphia, gesturing at the works with a dismissive hand.

Impey Barbicane, president of the Baltimore Gun Club, smiled. "You believe you will win your wager?"

"The money is mine, as surely as if it were already in my bank book."

The Baltimore Gun Club had been founded in the aftermath of the American Civil War in the 1860s. It was an organisation dedicated to the design of guns, cannons and artillery of all kinds. "It is guns that win wars, gentlemen," declared the Honourable Tom Hunter, one of the founding members. "It is guns that carried the day against the Confederacy. We must be sure that the United States retains the best guns, now and for the future!"

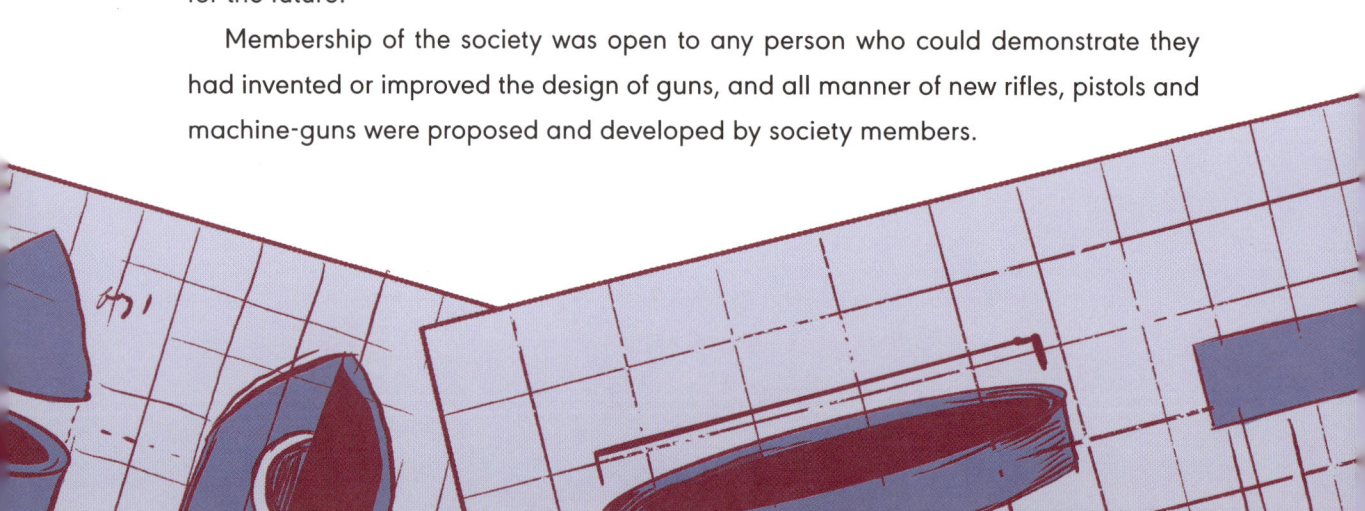

Membership of the society was open to any person who could demonstrate they had invented or improved the design of guns, and all manner of new rifles, pistols and machine-guns were proposed and developed by society members.

But for Barbicane, the society president, it was artillery rather than small arms that were what mattered. "It is the big guns, the cannons and mortars, that win wars," he insisted. "And, though we use them for war, that is not all of which they are capable. We can use cannons for peace as well as war."

"Peace?" queried Nicholl. He was a designer and manufacturer of plate armour, and was interested in the increase of the penetrating power of bullets. Cannons did not interest him. "What nonsense. Cannonballs have no civilian use!"

"On the contrary," said Barbicane. "Indeed, I have a proposal I intend to bring to the next general meeting of the society – to build a cannon of such dimensions that it can shoot a craft, and a crew of explorers, out of Earth altogether. We can use the cannon to explore the solar system!"

"Impossible!" scoffed Nicholl.

The proposal Barbicane put to the society was to build a cannon bigger than any attempted before: it would be situated in a 900-foot-deep and sixty-foot-wide circular hole, excavated in the side of a hill in Florida. Because the cannon could not be moved to aim it, the launch time would have to be synchronised with that moment when the target – the Moon – was in the right position in the sky. But there were many obstacles to be overcome before the capsule could be shot into the sky. Money would have to be raised to pay for the construction of the gun and its unique shell, and the excavation. The state of Florida would have to grant permission for the cannon to be constructed – there was a danger that the blast when the big gun was fired might be so huge it would split the ground in two like an earthquake.

"If I throw an apple in the air," Barbicane explained, "it will go up and then come down again. No matter how hard I pitch it, how fast I propel the apple, there is not enough force in my muscles to give it the speed it needs to escape Earth's gravitational pull altogether. The speed necessary is 12,000 yards a second! Seven miles a second – 25,000 miles per hour. To give our projectile such speed we will need many tons of the highest calibre gunpowder."

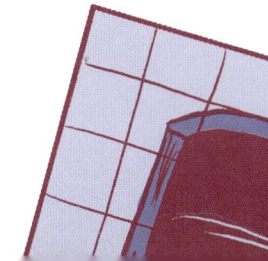

"But think of the shock of acceleration for those inside the capsule!" Nicholl exclaimed. "Surely it would kill them instantly."

"We will have to design the capsule to lessen the raw force of the acceleration," Barbicane agreed. "But hydraulic springs will absorb much of the shock, and though the passengers will experience a considerable force, they will survive. And once the capsule is travelling through space, they will not be aware of any sensation of motion at all – any more than we are aware we are in motion now, even though the Earth upon which we stand is rotating such that we are travelling at almost a thousand miles per hour."

"Will you actually land upon the Moon?" asked Michel Ardan, a young Frenchman who was visiting America and had become an associate member of the Gun Club.

"Not on this occasion," said Barbicane. "A landing would be possible, the same way we will land the capsule back on Earth at the end of its journey – by firing retroactive rockets to slow our descent. But were we to land on the Moon, how then would our explorers return? The Moon's gravity is much less than Earth's, barely a sixth of what we experience here, but nonetheless we would need some means of propelling the capsule back up into space. Building our cannon here will be challenge enough: building one upon the lunar surface would surely be too great a challenge. Still, our crew will be able to make closer observations of the Moon's surface than any previous scientist or astronomer ever has."

"Then I volunteer myself as a member of this crew!" said Ardan, with enthusiasm.

"It will be difficult, and likely dangerous," Barbicane cautioned him. "I cannot promise an easy or safe journey."

"I am not looking for safety or ease," Ardan returned, "but for adventure! I am willing to land the craft on the Moon."

"Land on the Moon?" scoffed Nicholl. "You forget, sir, that you would be hurtling towards the Moon inside a cannon-shell! Land on the Moon? You would crash into it, atomising yourself, and your only memorial would be a new crater for astronomers to peer at through their telescopes."

"I," said Ardan grandly, "am content to die, in order to be able to be the first human being to reach the Moon!"

"Noble – but insane!" exclaimed Nicholl.

Barbicane said, "My friend, you forget one thing: you will not be alone in the capsule. I myself will captain the voyage. And I have no intention of exploding myself to atoms! We shall equip the capsule with rockets that, facing forward, will slow our speed of descent. They would not be sufficient to lift us out of the Earth's immense gravity well, but they will enable us to land on the Moon safely, and to fly off it again when we have finished our exploring we will use these rockets to climb into space from the lunar surface."

"Mon capitaine!" Ardan stood to attention and saluted Barbicane.

"In addition to yourself," Barbicane added, "I will recruit one other crewman. Nicholl, might you be persuaded?"

Nicholl shook his head, laughing. "My dear Barbicane," he replied. "The entire project is unachievable. Your capsule will never launch. It's all so much poppycock!"

"I understand your caution," Barbicane replied.

This implication that Nicholl was declining to join the expedition out of cowardice touched a nerve. Stiffening, he returned, "On the contrary, my dear Barbicane: if your moon-ship were to fly, I would be delighted to be aboard. But I'll wager such an event will never come about."

"A thousand dollars?" Barbicane suggested.

"Done."

The two men shook hands.

And so work began. The first task was raising the money. Barbicane crafted a compelling manifesto seeking investment for the project and circulated it internationally. Just three days after the manifesto of President Barbicane, four million dollars were paid into the Baltimore Gun Club accounts. In the end, nearly five and a half million dollars were raised, pledged by all kinds of companies and private donors.

Nobody could have been more energetic or engaged than President Barbicane in overseeing the manufacture of the mighty barrel: the world's biggest metal tube, forged in the ironshops of the South. Barbicane purchased and oversaw the delivery of all the pig-iron and all the coke, and visited the forge daily. It seemed as if some mighty natural force was at work in the reddish vapours, the gigantic flames worthy of a volcano itself, these tremendous vibrations resembling the shock of an earthquake, these reverberations rivalling those of hurricanes and storms. But no: it was mankind that achieved this, his hand which precipitated into an abyss, dug by himself, a whole Niagara of molten metal!

From here the giant rings of steel were brought by cart to Stones Hill, Florida, where the pit was being excavated in which the cannon would be assembled and welded into a continuous tube. The task took eight months, and during the whole of this time Barbicane never quitted Stones Hill for a single instant. Keeping ever close by the work of excavation, he busied himself with the welfare and health of his workpeople.

The last piece of ironmongery was the making of the capsule itself – named the Columbiad, and cast as a whole, to ensure it had the strength to survive the shock of launch. The projectile was cast by Breadwill and Co., of Albany, and immediately forwarded by the Eastern Railway to Stones Hill, which it reached without accident on the tenth of November 1866, where Barbicane, Nicholl and Ardan were waiting impatiently for it.

The projectile was shaped like an artillery shell, but of gigantic size: 14 feet high and 8 feet in diameter. Built from aluminium, the walls, which would enclose and protect the inhabitants of the capsule, were 12 inches thick. Two portholes would allow for observation during the journey, offering a glimpse of the great expanse of space.

The interior was fitted with the necessities for life: the walls covered in padded leather, and sturdy couches around the edge of the capsule could be converted into beds. Heat and light were supplied by gas; food and water was loaded aboard.

As for the question of the air that would be consumed by Barbicane, his two companions and two dogs which he proposed taking with him: oxygen was supplied by tanks of compressed air, and the toxic carbon dioxide which the adventurers would breathe out rendered inert by means of chlorate of potassium and caustic potash stored in filters.

The whole compartment was placed within an outer skin in which water, diverted through various tubes and hydraulic run-offs, would act as a buffer to lessen the immense shock of departure. The travellers would still have to encounter a violent recoil when the cannon fired, but the springy escapement of this water would cushion it to render it survivable.

And now everything was in place, and launch set for the first of December. "Well, my friend," said Nicholl, writing a cheque for a thousand dollars and handing it to Barbicane. "You have won the bet."

"I shall lodge this with the Club accountant, and not cash it yet," Barbicane returned. "For we have yet to see whether the projectile will take flight."

The day of the launch arrived. An innumerable multitude covered the prairie around Stones Hill. Every quarter of an hour the railway brought fresh accessions of sightseers. For a month previously, the mass of these persons had bivouacked round the enclosure, covering the plain with huts, cottages and tents. The whole world had been following Barbicane's project; all the various classes of American society had assembled in terms of absolute equality to observe the launch: bankers, farmers, sailors, cotton-planters, brokers, merchants, watermen and magistrates elbowed each other in the most free-and-easy way.

Barbicane, Nicholl and Ardan and the two dogs entered the capsule and closed the hatch. It was then lowered by crane into the vast cylinder of the cannon, and the crowds were ushered away from the pit.

J T Maston, the Gun Club secretary, was afforded the honour of pressing with his finger the key of the electric battery to discharge the spark into the breech and so fire the Columbiad.

He counted down and, upon reaching zero, he depressed the button.

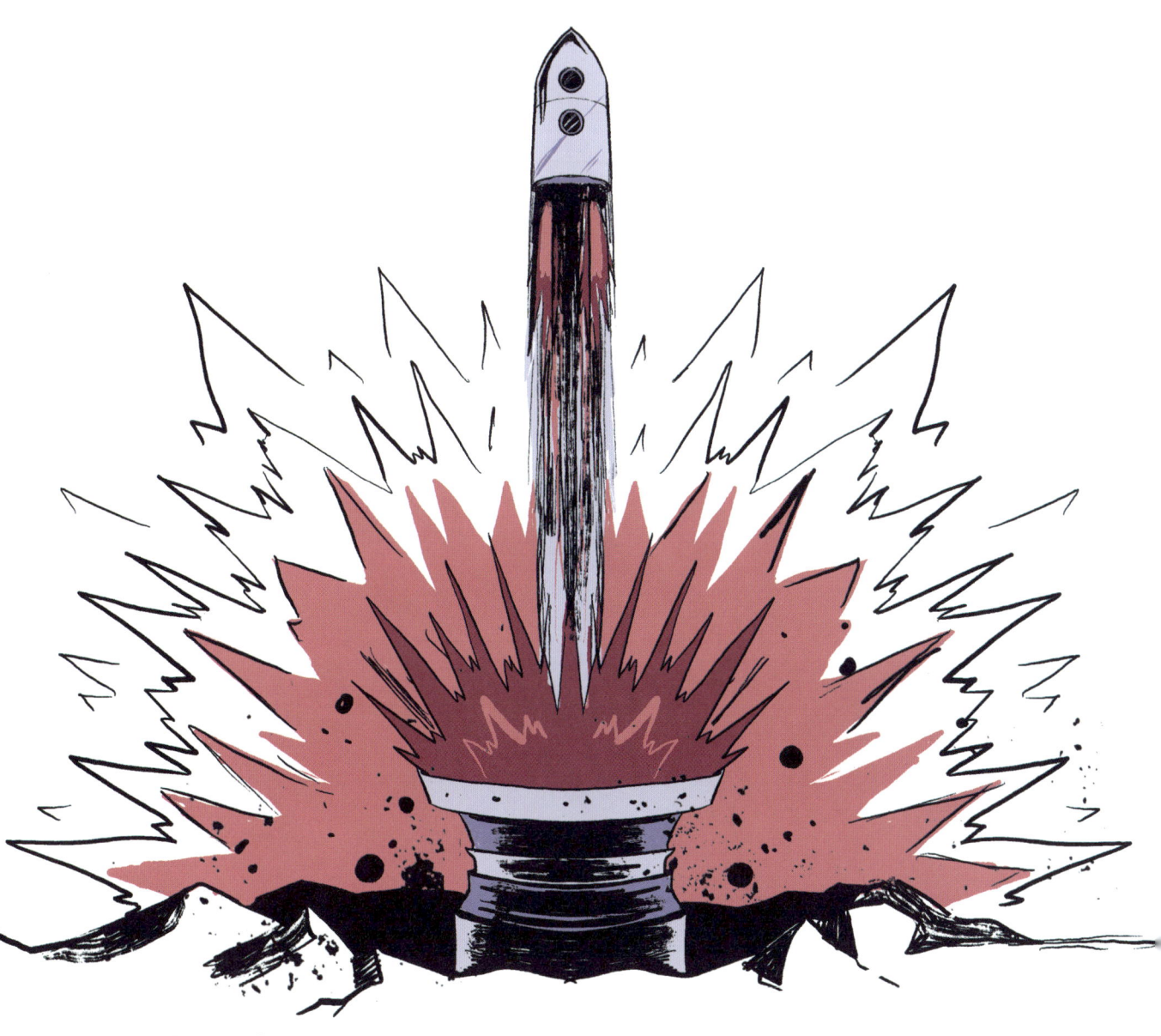

An appalling unearthly report followed instantly. An immense spout of fire shot up from the bowels of the Earth as from a crater, and the spectators obtained a momentary glimpse of the projectile victoriously cleaving the air in the midst of the fiery vapours.

A pyramid of fire rose to a prodigious height into the air, the glare of flame lit up the whole of Florida, and for a moment day superseded night over a considerable extent of the country.

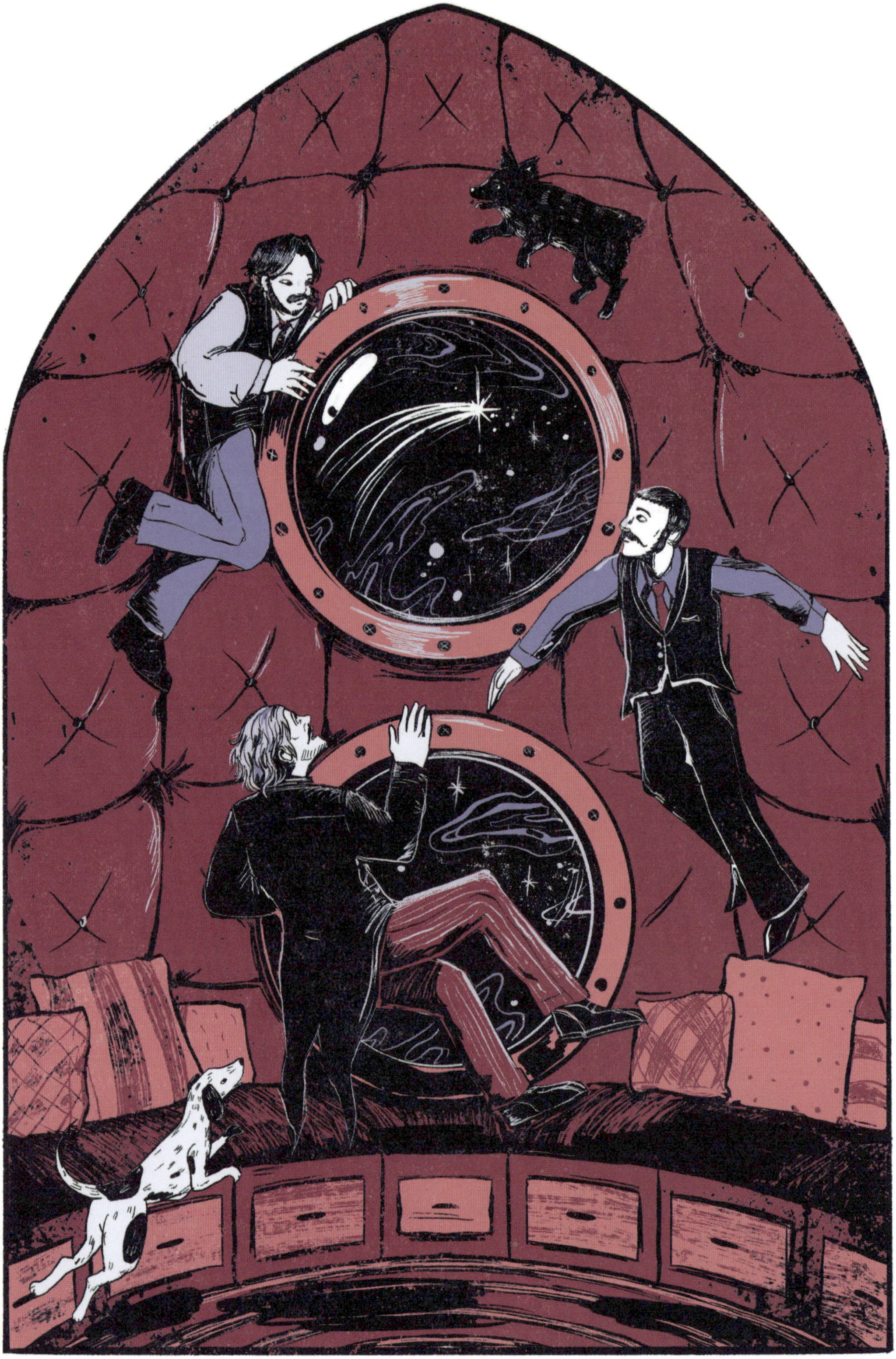

Inside the capsule, the three crewmembers, stunned and shaken by the immense jolt of launch, roused themselves. The dogs, whimpering at the noise and shock, licked their hands. "We're away!" Barbicane announced.

"You shall be able to cash my cheque after all!" said Nicholl.

"For that we shall have to survive our journey, our landing on the Moon and our return," cautioned Barbicane. "It will take us five days even to reach our target, so great is the distance between the Earth and Moon."

"And what will we find there?" Ardan wondered. "Life? Lunar cows and lunar sheep? Lunar dogs?" He scratched the heads of their two hounds.

"We shall see," said Barbicane. "Though I suspect any life that has developed upon the Moon will be in kind quite different to Earthly beings."

Ardan opened the shutters on one of the lenticular portholes, and the three men peered out. The Earth beneath them showed a crescent finely traced on the dark background of the sky, the line rendered bluish by the stratum of the atmosphere. Up ahead of the travellers, as if trying to pierce the profound darkness, a brilliant cluster of shooting stars burst upon their eyes: hundreds of meteorites, ignited by the friction of the atmosphere, irradiating the shadow.

"See!" Ardan exclaimed. "It is as if nature herself is celebrating our departure with her most brilliant fireworks!"

The meteors burned out, but then a single, much larger asteroid came shooting towards them. It seemed at first as if it might collide with and destroy the Columbiad, and Ardan cried out in alarm. It passed within a few hundred yards, and the three men watched its huge, mottled flank as it swept by.

"The asteroid had been captured by the Earth's gravity," Barbicane declared, "and has become a second moon! See, it moves on in an orbital trajectory."

"I am only glad that it did not collide with us," said Nicholl. "It would surely have broken us into a thousand pieces."

The capsule hurtled onwards, through the emptiness of space, and Mother Earth shrank from a great arc to a large circle, and then a smaller disc.

Inside the confines of the capsule, the three men slept, and ate, and made observations, gazing out into the empty expanse of space. And with every hour the Moon, towards which they sped, grew in size.

Of the two dogs, one recovered its spirits and was as lively as ever, but the other remained in a depressed state. Nicholl, examining it, pronounced that it had been badly bruised and its bones broken during the launch. The poor dog quickly slackened and soon passed away.

"I grieve for our brave comrade!" declared Ardan, with tears in his eyes. They held the first casualty of the voyage against the glass of the lenticular porthole, and pulled the lever to angle it, opening it a couple of inches. The difference between the airy pressure inside the compartment and the empty vacuum of space pulled the body swiftly out, and Barbicane leant on the lever to close the porthole. A turn of the dial on one of the air cylinders soon replaced any air that had been lost.

On the third day, Nicholl, his spirits restored, observing at one of the windows, reported that their destination had moved. "The Moon, which has been in the centre of the window's view, is further to the left."

"Indeed," said Barbicane. "Though it is not the Moon that has moved, but us. Evidently the gravitational force of our earlier encounter with the asteroid has caused our projectile to deviate from its course. Gentlemen, we will not be able to land upon the Moon!"

"Must we then miss the Moon and so pass out into emptiness, to travel forever – and to our death?" demanded Nicholl. "Cursed be the meteor which crossed our path and brought with it such a dire fate!"

"You forget, my friend, that the Moon has a gravitational attraction that will draw us, either into an orbit around her, or perhaps to swing us back towards the Earth."

"I ask but one thing," said Ardan, "that we may pass near enough to penetrate her secrets."

Barbicane took observations and made calculations in order to better ascertain the trajectory of the capsule, which propelled onwards through the dark nothingness.

By the fifth day, as the Moon filled the portholes, it was clear that they would circumnavigate her globe at a height of some five hundred miles. The three men watched eagerly as they flew over the crater of Eratosthenes and a chain of lunar mountains at the twentieth lunar parallel.

The land below was uninhabited – a desert of grey sand and darker rocks. There was no sign of life. "Neither lunar sheep, cow nor dog," Nicholl observed, "I'm sorry to report, Michel."

They passed over an area of great parallel rifts in the lunar surface: almost, Ardan declared, as if long lines of fortifications had been raised by Selenite engineers. But there was nothing moving, nothing that spoke of life in that desolate landscape.

Soon enough the craft passed behind the Moon, flying over the 'dark side' which is never spied from Earth. It was not dark from lack of illumination, however, for the sunlight shone strongly upon one half of it. The three men were most eager to observe what no human eyes had ever seen before.

At first they saw a surface much like the other side of the globe: hills, craters, lines. But then they passed over an immense plain, littered with countless white objects glinting in the sunlight. In awe, the men cast their eyes down upon the far side of the moon, an ancient mystery that had been hidden from man for millions of years, until now.

"Might those be white marble fragments?" Nicholl suggested. "Thrown, perhaps, pell-mell, by some lunar volcano? They are so very numerous!"

"It seems to me," replied Michel quietly, "that rather than marble shards, they are bones. This plain would then be nothing but an immense cemetery, upon which repose the mortal remains of thousands of extinct generations."

Eventually they passed beyond the plain and into the half of the globe in darkness: lunar night. Now nothing could be discerned. Soon they would swing round and travel along the parabola back towards Earth. Michel was lamenting that they could see nothing when a single meteorite burst with light, landing and breaking up into hot, bright fragments.

It afforded the three men a glimpse – the briefest of glances – of a world: immense spaces, no longer arid plains, but real seas, oceans, widely distributed, reflecting on their liquid surface all the dazzling magic of the fires of space; and, lastly, on the surface of the continents, large dark masses, looking like immense forests under the rapid illumination of a brilliance. Was it an illusion? Could they give a scientific assent to an observation so superficially obtained? Dared they pronounce upon the question of its habitability after only a glimpse of the invisible disc?

"Life!" exclaimed Ardan. "We must land – can we not fire our rockets, slow our passage and sink onto the surface of that world?"

"Our trajectory has been disarranged," Barbicane explained. "We are no longer simply heading towards the Moon, where de-acceleration would enable us to land. Firing the rockets now would embroil us in complex parabolas and curlicues. It might be possible to calculate a path down to the surface of the Moon, but it would require complicated mathematical calculation and much time."

Ardan, impetuous and eager to explore the surface, heard only it might be possible, and rushed to the button that controlled the rockets. Before Barbicane could call out 'No!' he had ignited the rockets. The travellers were jolted as the rocket slowed, but then, under the oblique influence of the Moon's gravity the capsule spun and lurched, propelled away from, rather than towards, the Moon. As they spiralled away, Barbicane hurried to the controls, cut off the full blast of all rockets, and – as the capsule rotated like a fairground ride – isolated one rocket and ignited it to quench their spinning. Then, glancing out the portholes at the receding surface of the Moon, Ardan fired a different rocket and sent the capsule sweeping in back towards the Moon, skimming the shoulder of the disc and flying on back towards the Earth at a higher speed.

Ardan, watching the Moon recede from the rearward window, moaned. "Apologies, my comrades! I achieved the opposite of what I intended."

He saluted the departing Moon. "Farewell, mysterious world! Perhaps one day we will return."

"Since we are now hurtling back into the immense gravitational attraction of Earth,"

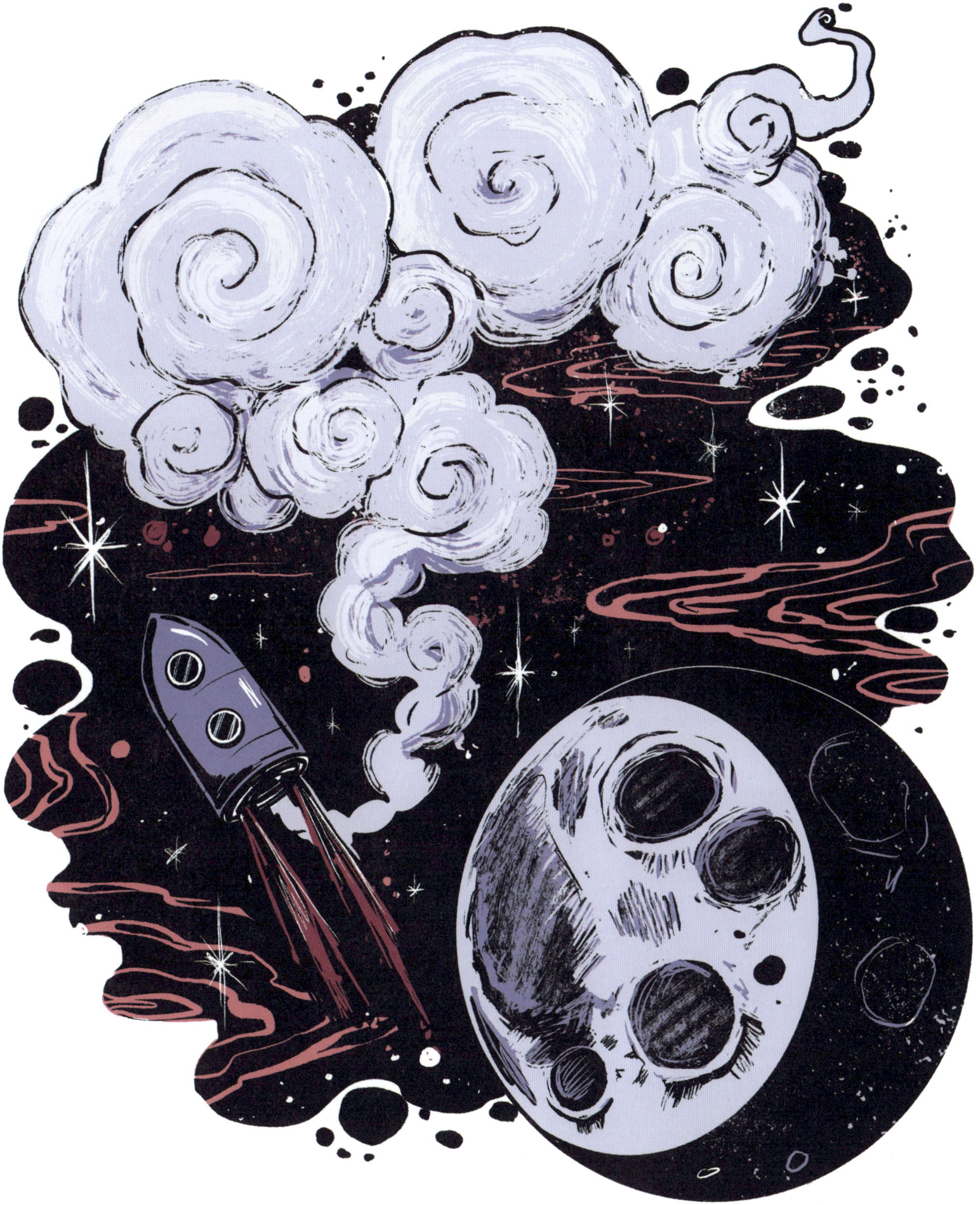

Barbicane noted, "having used up all our rocketry for de-accelerating, I fear that whoever returns to explore the Moon herself will not be us."

His two comrades hurried to assist as Barbicane undertook difficult mathematical calculations, numbers and diagrams. Their fate was out of their hands: they would arrive at the Earth travelling at much greater speeds than they had anticipated, and without the rocket power to quench their velocity. "We must pray we land upon water and not upon land – for on land we will assuredly be dashed to pieces!"

"But if we land in the ocean," Nicholl asked, "will we not sink into the depths?"

"We must hope that Earth-based observatories are watching our approach. We will appear to their telescopes as a large and rapid meteor, and if – as I hope we do – we land in the sea, perhaps they will be able to have a ship nearby such that we can be rescued before we sink."

"If we are rescued," said Nicholl, "then I will be glad to relinquish the money I have lost in my wager. And if we are not – well, then it hardly matters!"

There was now nothing to do but wait. Hour by hour the Earth grew larger and more beautiful: a mosaic of blues and greens and yellows, overlaced with a thousand ribbons of white cloud. The craft was quiet for some time.

"You do not regret agreeing to join the expedition, my friend?" Barbicane asked Nicholl.

"It has been the adventure of my life!" Nicholl replied. "However it ends, I am delighted to be here. You have certainly proved the efficacy of the larger design of cannon!"

"My friend," Barbicane mused, as he watched the great disc of the Earth through the capsule's window. "I am thinking now of an even greater cannon. Consider: our Earth rotates at an angle of some twenty-four degrees. Because of this slant rotation, the poles are freezing and the equator too hot. Imagine if we could reconfigure this spin! If the Earth were to spin on a perfectly vertical axis, all areas of the world would receive the same portion of sunlight, everywhere from north pole to south would become temperate – fertile, hospitable. It would open up millions of hectares of land to habitation and so ease the pressures that lead to war."

"And how would you achieve so titanic a change?"

"Simply by building the biggest gun – a cannon to which the one that launched us would be a mere pop-gun. By orienting the barrel and firing a projectile of sufficient weight, the recoil would shock the Earth itself into a more regular rotation!"

"Amazing!" said Nicholl. "Of course, we must first survive our return..."

Unknown to the crew, back on Earth the projectile was being closely watched through the largest telescopes in America and round the world. When it was seen that the mission had failed to land upon the Moon, and was in fact off course and hurtling back towards the Earth, the members of the Baltimore Gun Club convened a meeting. They were discussing how to contact the members of the crew, and what could be done to guide the projectile to a safe landing, when J M Belfast, director of the Cambridge observatory, burst in. "The projectile!" he cried. "It has fallen to the Earth!"

"You're sure that cursed projectile has fallen?" asked J T Maston, the secretary.

"Into the Pacific!"

"Then there is no time to lose."

They immediately contacted colleagues on the other side of the country, in Los Angeles, instructing them to charter a ship and begin searching for the fallen capsule. "You had better make it a trawler," said Belfast. "Who knows from what depths we will have to drag up this projectile."

"And how long the crew can survive underwater. They will have some air but not much – for they will have used up almost all their supply on the mission. And their craft is designed for the vacancy of space, not the intense pressures at the bottom of the Pacific!"

The cable was sent, and a reply received, and the very next day a craft set out from the Californian coast.

A week passed, and the members of the club waited anxiously for news to arrive via telegram. But there was no news. Three members took the railroad all the way across America, to be on the ground when – if – the fallen cannonball was found and brought to the surface. But, they cabled ruefully, nothing had been found.

"My calculations," said Belfast, "suggest that their air will all have been used up by now, and our brave travellers must be dead."

Suddenly, there was a shout from J T Maston. "What idiots we have been!" he cried. "How heavy is this projectile?"

"19,250 pounds in weight. Enough to sink rapidly to the ocean bottom."

"But you forget it is hollow and full of air. It may weigh 19,250 pounds, but it displaces 56,000 pounds – twenty-eight tons."

"And so—"

"And so it floats!"

And it was true! All – yes! all – these savants had forgotten this fundamental law; namely that on account of its displacement and the buoyancy of its hollow interior, the projectile must, having plunged into the water, bob up again like a cork to float upon the surface.

A cable was immediately dispatched, and a second boat sent to find the first with instructions not to trawl the seabed but to search the surface.

Within hours the projectile was found, bobbing on the waves. One of the scuttles of the projectile was open, above the waterline. Some pieces of glass remained in the frame, showing that it had been broken. A boat came alongside and at that moment was heard a clear and merry voice, the voice of Ardan, exclaiming in an accent of triumph: "White all, Barbicane, white all!"

Barbicane, Ardan and Nicholl were playing at dominoes.

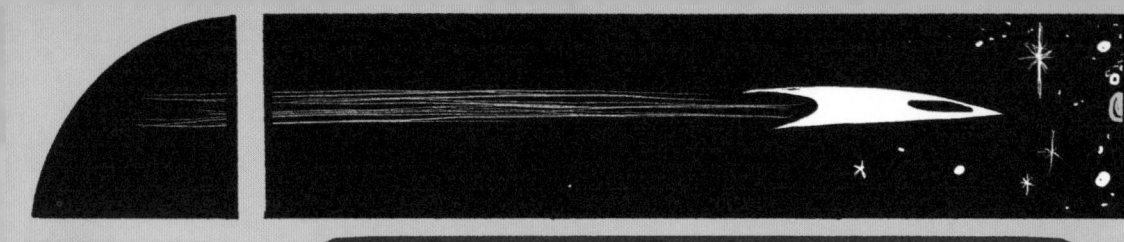

A JOURNEY INTO THE UNKNOWN

The dream of travelling off Earth is very old. In the second century AD, Lucian Samosata imagined a storm at sea powerful enough to lift a ship into the air and all the way to the Moon. Johannes Kepler's *Somnium* (1632) has a lunar explorer carried on the back of a flying witch; William Godwin's *The Man in the Moone* (1638) imagines a man carried to the Moon by a flock of geese; the protagonist of Edgar Allan Poe's *Hans Pfaall* (1835) flies to the Moon in a hot-air balloon. These tales are jolly but, obviously, impracticable.

An influential and prolific author, Jules Verne was a rationalist, a practical man whose science fictional extrapolations stuck, as far as possible, to scientific plausibility... at least up to a point. H G Wells wrote a novel (*The First Men in the Moon*, 1901) in which explorers fly to the Moon in a ship powered by anti-gravity. But, Verne pointed out, there's no such thing as anti-gravity, which he thought rendered the book invalid – mere fantasy. When Verne wrote his story about lunar explorers, he grounded it in the real science of his day. In the 1860s, there was only one way Verne could imagine a spacecraft being launched so as to escape the Earth's gravitational pull: it must be fired out of a giant cannon.

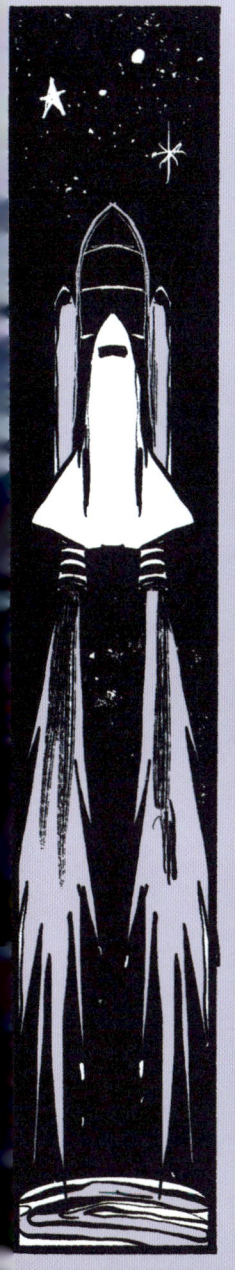

A cannonball fired upwards needs to travel at a speed of 40,287 kilometres per hour (25,020 miles per hour) to achieve escape velocity. If it's travelling any slower than this, it will fall back to the ground. Scientists before Verne had worked this out, so Verne applied it to his story. A gun large enough to fire a cannonshell at such prodigious speeds would be very large indeed, and Verne's tale explains how it came to be made, and what happened when it was fired. This attention to scientific accuracy was brought into science fiction by Verne. Yet it only goes so far. In fact, a projectile fired from a cannon at such a speed would burn up at once, because of the intense friction it would experience passing through the lower atmosphere. Plus, think of the human crew inside the projectile. Accelerating from zero to over 40,000 kilometres per hour in an instant would turn them into a smear of strawberry jam on the rear wall of the compartment. Verne tries to address this by suggesting that his craft is fitted with hydraulic pistons and levers to deaden the brute force of the acceleration – but this still wouldn't come anywhere near working. Today, we use rockets to lift our astronauts into space because they accelerate slowly though the lower air and only reach escape velocity much higher up. But rockets were not a viable part of Verne's world. He does the best he can with the science and technology available to him at the time. And though the words 'in fact' have been used in this paragraph, a story is not a fact: it's a story. And this story works very well.

THE WAR OF THE WORLDS

It began with lights flickering upon the surface of Mars. Observatories across Europe beheld these gleams through their telescopes, and reports were posted in scientific journals. There were even brief notices in some newspapers. There was speculation: perhaps the lights indicated volcanic activity. Perhaps they were even signs of life.

Had we understood what those flickering lights meant, we would have splashed the news across every headline in the world! The lights were the muzzle-flashes of gigantic guns, firing projectiles into space. As we went about our lives, oblivious, those projectiles were hurtling through space, coming ever closer to Earth.

Shall I ever forget the night the Martians arrived?

For months, life went on as it always had. I was living at that time in Surrey, on the outskirts of London town. I was recently married, and my wife was asleep downstairs. I was in my study upstairs, working on some writing - how foolish and trivial my occupation seems now, as I look back on it with hindsight! - and the casement window was open. It was a warm summer night, a great spread of stars shining with their diamond light, and the scent of the lobelias strong in the balmy air. Away towards Woking I could hear the chiming and clanking of railway cars coupling and uncoupling, and rolling along their rails, distance making the clamour melodic. I happened to look up and see the meteor - or so I thought it - flare across the black sky, like a match being dragged and lit. It hurtled brightly down, landing somewhere beyond the trees.

I even felt the tremble in the Earth from its impact.

Excited to see the crater it had made, and whether any of it had survived the impact, I took a coat and stepped outside. It was a short journey by bicycle over dark roads through the woods and out onto Horsell Common, for that is where the thing had landed.

I was not the first person to arrive: a small crowd had gathered on the common with lanterns, and they had come to see the meteorite. A fire had been lit, and the combination of firelight, lamplight and moonlight shone on the ridge of a newly made crater.

I laid my bicycle on the ground and joined a dozen other people on the edge of this crater. At the bottom of the hollow was no meteorite, but rather a smooth steel cylinder, two dozen yards in length and ten yards in diameter at the ends. It was gleaming, heated by its passage through the Earth's atmosphere, and as it cooled it emitted snaps and cracks, like sticks being broken.

"That's no meteorite!" I exclaimed.

"It is," the man standing next to me declared, holding his lantern up the better to illuminate the scene, "the queerest thing I ever did see."

"Look!" cried another voice. "The end – it's turning."

The top end of the cylinder was indeed rotating, making a deep scraping noise as it turned. It moved slowly round one complete cycle, and then a second. As it did so, it lifted, and it was possible to see the large screw grooves by which it was fitted into the main body of the cylinder. With each turn it came up further until, finally, it came free and tumbled away. No sooner was the cylinder opened than something emerged from it.

You may have seen a Martian: if you are old enough to remember the invasion you will perhaps have observed one in a museum or on display. The British Museum has a nearly complete specimen, preserved in a great glass tank filled with formaldehyde. But nothing could convey to you the sheer horror of seeing them in motion. Their giant heads and flat, grey saucer eyes; their skin black and glistening like an octopus, or a bear coated in tar; the beak-like mouths, constantly in motion; the tentacles that hang from their undersides, writhing and curling and reaching. We now know that they have no bodies, for evolution on their world has done away with torsos and limbs, with stomachs and digestive tracts. They do not eat food and extract nutrition from it as we do; rather they ingest blood from other animals and pass it about their circulatory system, and that contains all the necessaries for life. They are giant brains, and instead of hands they have tentacles with which to manipulate.

For a moment I laid eyes on a Martian and gasped in horror. It seemed to be struggling – for, of course, the gravity of Earth is much greater than that of Mars, and the effort of climbing out of the cylinder must have been immense. The creature struggled at the edge and then fell out, tumbling into the shadows.

The man next to me cried, "It is suffering – it needs help!" and immediately began clambering into the crater, his lantern light bobbing downwards.

I could not see where the Martian had fallen, but I saw what happened next clearly. The man caught fire. A ray of pure heat, fired from the cylinder, struck him, passed through his body and struck the crater wall not far from me, making the mud boil and bubble. The poor fellow did not even have time to cry out: his chest was vaporised and the rest of his body burned in a fierce flame. The lantern fell to the ground. There was a moment of silence.

Somebody cried out in horror.

Down in the pit there was movement: metal tentacles writhed, stretched, reached up with purpose. I could see that each held a box-like device, and that these were the sources of the invisible heat ray. As the tentacles curled and lifted, these weapons angled and pointed, looking for new targets.

Having aimed their ray at this one person, the Martians turned it and shot down another person standing on the lip of the crater. The heat ray struck another person, and then another, and only then did the crowd understand what was happening. There was screaming and shouts of outrage, and people fled, running away from the crater in all directions. I stumbled back as the heat ray passed near me, scalding the air – I could sense the warmth and smell the burnt ozone smell. Then I ran. I tripped, got up, struggled on, found my bicycle and got away.

All the way back to my house my mind was hurrying, working through the implications of what I had seen. One thing above all was clear: the area was not safe. At home I woke our maid and roused my wife.

"You must get away from here," I told her.

"My darling, but why? What has happened?"

I gave her a brief account of the events at the crater. "Go to Leatherhead – go straight to my cousin's house, and take the baby. I will join you in a day or two."

"I must go without you?"

"I will make necessary arrangements here, and lock up the house. And I shall write a report for the *Times* – but I will come as soon as I can."

As we brought the pony out of its stable and harnessed it to the gig, the roads were busy. The army had been summoned, and troops of soldiers, horses and cannons were marching towards Horsell Common. "See," said my wife. "The military have this strange arrival in hand! They will quell its danger."

"When they do, my love, you may return and we can continue with our life." And so I kissed her, and she and Jenny the maid rode away into the dawn.

That night, I wrote an account of the strange arrival and telegraphed it to the offices of the *Times*. By the time I had done all that, it was fully light. Though I had not slept I was too excited to rest, and made my way back up onto the common.

Despite the carnage of the night before, a crowd had gathered. The army had set up camp, and artillery had been positioned, aimed at the cylinder. Troops were keeping civilians away from the crater itself.

"Have you heard?" a young fellow asked me, as I arrived. "Another of these things has landed – north of Reading. They say there have been seven in all, across the country."

"Have these other creatures fired their death ray?" I asked. "Are there more casualties?"

"Not they," the man said heartily. "Now that the soldiers are here, I'd say they've thought twice about making a nuisance of themselves. Let them only try it! Those big guns will make short work of them." He seemed hectic with confidence. The mood of the crowd was strangely jolly, like a carnival.

"Such clanging and banging!" said a woman nearby.

"What's that?"

"All night," she said, "there's been a regular clatter out of that there crater. It sounds like they're a-building something, I say."

And now a soldier was advancing on the crater holding a flag of truce. It seemed as if negotiations were about to commence. "Now we'll see!" said the hectic fellow. "They'll be cowed by our guns, alright! Those monsters."

Something rose up out of the crater. It lifted itself above the lip and kept on growing: my first ever sight of a Martian's war machine. This is what they had been building through the night! A huge metal hood covered the cockpit of the device, and raised up upon gigantic legs – three of them, jointed and articulate, lifting the whole machine a hundred feet into the air. The main hood had window-like shapes across its front, its empty eyes that glowed eerily directed their gaze on the lines of soldiers below.

The crowd gasped. The tripod flexed its legs and stepped up out of the crater. Towering above us, it let loose a gigantic noise, a cacophonous hooting shriek that nearly broke my eardrums and made me physically quail.

At the front of the hood, atop the mighty legs, was a box-like device, held in metal tentacles. This the Martian inside aimed at the nearest of the army's cannons, and fired down its heat ray. The gun exploded, and I looked on in disbelief as flames quickly engulfed the front line of defence.

The soldiers scurried and ran, struggling to right their cannons, all aimed into the pit, to bear on this new target. But they were too slow! The giant tripod stepped easily amongst them, shooting its heat ray at this gun and that, and in moments the artillery was all destroyed. Only one gun got off a shot, and it whistled past the tripod's legs and fell away into the far reaches of the common.

Now everything was chaos. Soldiers took up position, aiming their rifles and firing. The civilians were swarming away, screaming and shouting, running for their lives. I heard the snap of rifle fire and the ping as bullets bounced off the metal hood of the Martian machine, but I too was running, lumbering up a slope and away.

It was going uphill that saved my life, for the Martian tripod now deployed a second weapon: a noxious black smoke pouring out of the rear of its cockpit, sinking through the air and asphyxiating all upon whom it fell. By the time I had reached the top of the hill I looked down upon a terrible scene: the black smoke was everywhere in the hollow, roiling like a foul mist, and all human resistance had been extinguished.

From the Martian tripod came an awful, howling cry, loud enough to bowl me over. I pressed my hands to my ears but the sound penetrated: *ullaaaaah!*

I stumbled away from the common, the horrible shrieks of the Martian splitting the air behind me.

My bicycle was lost. My clothes were covered in dirt. I hid behind a wall for a while to catch my breath and listened: screams, crashes, the cackling sound of burning buildings, the thud of tripods – for there were several now – stomping about the countryside, and again and again the cries of *ullaaaaah!*

Looking above the wall I could see the tops of three of the Martians' giant tripod machines. They were stalking eastward – towards London – stopping to aim their heat ray at a target, or to discharge another cloud of the deadly black smoke. Everywhere I could see buildings on fire, gashes in the landscape, ruin.

An artilleryman, his uniform torn and scorched, dived behind the wall and fell across me. "Were you on the common?" I asked.

"Wiped out!" he said. "My whole battalion gone. I was lucky to escape – hid under a dead horse until I could make a run for it."

"How can we fight such monsters?"

"We can't!" he sobbed. "Wiped out!" Peering over the top of the wall, he suddenly yelled with fright: "Coming this way!"

Together we scurried away, keeping as low as we could, running across gardens, down alleys. I did not recognise where I was until we came out upon the river and I saw that we were near Weybridge. People were evacuating the town, dragging their belongings in handcarts or hauling them on their backs. The bridge was crowded.

"This is the wrong way. I have to get to Leatherhead," I told the soldier. "My wife is there – I must get to her."

"There's the army," he cried, pointing. On the northern bank of the Thames, a mass of uniformed men had assembled, waiting behind sandbag walls, and aiming their big guns upriver. "I'll go that way – I'll see if any of my platoon has survived."

I bade him farewell, and watched as he jogged across the bridge.

Then, from upriver, I heard the ghastly call of an approaching Martian. Round the river bend they came: three of the huge machines, striding through the water, wavelets splashing as their legs moved. I heard the shouts of the military commander from across the bridge, readying his men for the assault, and saw the gunners swivel and target their guns.

We got the first shot off. A whoosh and crash, and a great spout of water beside the nearest of the tripods. In a flash, three tripods directed their heat rays at the battery, and the whole encampment seemed to explode in a firework display of flame and brightness and spirals of smoke. The noise was extraordinary, hideous, and the shock passing through the air knocked me over, even though I was on the far side of the river. As I scrambled back up I saw the last remaining troops shooting their rifles, and one last cannon firing, reloading, taking aim and firing again.

This last shell struck the underside of the hood of the nearmost tripod. There was a sharp blast, a great retort, and the top of the tripod broke open in a tangled mass of metal. The tripod stopped dead, a tower of smoke pouring upwards from its ruined top: it swayed, and then crashed down with a colossal splash of water and steam.

I could hear the cheers of the surviving solders, and almost cheered myself. But the remaining tripods immediately fired their heat rays and the big gun was instantly destroyed. The cheer stuck in my throat. Then, as the two surviving tripods continued their advance, I turned and ran. Behind me they were depositing their noisome toxic smoke onto the water, where it roiled and rolled like a black fog. Terror took me that I would breathe this in and expire then and there: I ran as fast as my legs could take me, the edge of the stench of the stuff tickling my nostrils, until I was able to struggle up a hill and breathe fresher air. Finally I collapsed, panting and exhausted.

Eventually I made my way to Leatherhead through a landscape pitted with craters and broken houses. Already the countryside was starting to change: for, as you know, the Martians brought with them the red weed, the vast fields of which give their home planet its distinctive colour. Under the brighter Sun and more fertile soil of Earth, this weed proliferated; within days it was growing everywhere, choking rivers and swamping fields.

On a rise on the outskirts of Leatherhead I saw the whole town burning. I wept, but did not stay – a tripod was stalking through the smoke and ashes in the distance and I did not want to attract its attention. Perhaps, I told myself, my wife had escaped the town before the Martians destroyed it.

For several days I roamed the countryside, taking such provisions as I could: stale bread from an abandoned bakery here, water from a town pump there. At some point in west London I came to the Thames again. Red weed grew prolifically from both banks, its scarlet tendrils waving in the stream. All the buildings were broken, and some still smoked.

There were tripods everywhere. Each of the Martian cylinders – for many had landed, in a spread across southern England – must have brought with it the materials for building multiple such machines, and now Martians were piloting them in an orgy of destruction and conquest. There seemed nothing we humans could do to stop it.

I was, I believe, somewhere near Walton when a phalanx of tripods surprised me with a huge *ullah*! They were marching eastward, heading into central London, and their passage would take them close by me. Panicking, I ran, found a house still half-standing and scrambled inside. I watched them through the window – its glass all shattered and gone – until they came closer still and I hurried down into the house's basement.

It was there that I met a curate, a figure in soot-smudged shirt sleeves, and with his upturned, clean-shaven face staring at the light from the open cellar door above him. "I thought it might be one of them!" he gasped as I descended.

"Do they come into houses?" I asked.

"They have machines that do so," the curate said. "Some of us they kill, but others they capture and take away. I have seen what becomes of such unfortunates! Kept in cages until their blood is entirely drained away – bled dry to feed these monsters!"

For a while we were silent, listening to the thumps and earthen shudder that marked the passage of the tripods. There was one final *ullah!* and then silence.

We introduced one another. The curate had been hiding in the cellar for two days, darting out from time to time to source supplies where he could. "There's a tap," he said, "which is still producing water – I don't know for how long. I've managed to gather some tins, and some packets of dry biscuits. There's oil to keep this lantern alight for a few more days, then we must get some more."

He shared what he had with me, and for a while we simply talked. He had fled the church at Weybridge when the attack began, hidden under hedges and inside ruined houses. One sunset, he had witnessed what he mentioned: Martians feeding greedily on the blood of human captives. They had (or their machines had) excavated a kind of pit and there, on beds of red weed, the hideous creatures had each taken a human – a man, a woman, a child, they were indifferent – from certain cages in which they kept their prisoners, pierced their necks or chests with a feeding pipe and drew up their blood. To have seen so horrible a sight had marked the curate. I began to understand that it had, in a sense, broken him.

"How long do you intend to remain here?"

"Until it is safe to go out again!" he replied.

But it began to dawn on me that, for the curate, it would never be safe. "I have also," he confided, "liberated a few bottles of claret wine." I was happy to share one such with him, but under the influence of the alcohol he became immensely maudlin.

"Why does God permit these Martians to afflict us?" he complained. "What sins have we done? Everywhere – fire, earthquake, death! What are these Martians?"

"What are we?" I answered, clearing my throat.

He began waving his hands. "All the work – all the Sunday schools. What have we done? What has Weybridge done? Everything gone – everything destroyed. The church! We rebuilt it only three years ago. Gone! Swept out of existence! Why?" Now he was weeping, despairing, shouting that God had abandoned us. It was very grating.

Still, I did not choose at that time to leave the cellar. I wish I had! For several days I stayed there, listening to the ceaseless moaning and imprecations of the curate. It increasingly got on my nerves, but each time I ventured up the stairs and peered through the glassless window I saw more flames bursting out and tripods stalking to and fro, and hurried back below.

My main fear during that period was that a tripod would unleash a quantity of the black smoke in the vicinity, and that the curate and I would choke to death like rats in a trap. But my fear of this was not enough to winkle me out of the space. I think, in retrospect, I was hiding to avoid not the Martians, so much as the thought that I had lost my wife in the chaos.

Matters came to a head. Now that I was there, the curate no longer felt the need to venture out to retrieve supplies. I went instead, and the curate sank deeper into a kind of insanity of despair. Everything was hopeless, he wailed. We had driven God away with our sinfulness. There was no point in anything. "I am as great a sinner as any!" he cried. "I have sinned!"

The sound of Martian tripods marching nearby could be heard inside the cellar. I begged him to be quiet, to lie still until the tripods had gone. But this only aggravated his insanity. "No," he yelled. "I must pray! I must exorcise these devils!"

Before I could stop him, he had scrambled up the cellar stairs. I went after him but could not stop him running outside the house and standing before one of the huge Martian machines. "The word of God is upon me!" he cried. "Get thee behind me, Satan!"

I watched from the window, expecting the Martian to annihilate him with a heat ray. But instead a metallic tentacle snaked from the hood of the tripod, grasped the curate and lifted him into the air. As I watched in horror, the tripod walked away with giant strides, the curate's screams diminishing with the distance.

I could no longer stay in that cellar. Weeping, desperate, I ran from the house and staggered through the ruins of the town. It was pure luck I avoided being seen by the Martians and sharing the curate's ghastly fate. I dashed from wall to hedge, running behind smoking, broken houses, trying to put distance between myself and the shrieking tripods. Everywhere I went was ruined. There were many bodies, tangling together in death, many stained sooty with the remnants of the black smoke that had killed them.

I found myself in Fulham, entirely alone. The streets were horribly quiet. For a while I rested, got my breath back. There was black dust all along the roadways. I found food – sour, hard and mouldy, but edible – out of a baker's shop. Some way towards Walham Green the streets became clear of black powder, and I passed a white terrace of houses on fire; the noise of the burning was almost a relief. Going on towards Brompton, the streets were quiet again.

Now that I knew where I was, I directed my steps towards the centre of London. I am not sure why: perhaps I wanted to see how our mighty capital fared – the centre of the country, the heart of everything. Perhaps some resistance had been mounted? Perhaps consolidated force was driving the Martians back?

The further I penetrated into London, the profounder grew the stillness – it was the stillness of suspense, of expectation. It was near South Kensington that I first heard the howling. It crept almost imperceptibly upon my senses. It was a sobbing alternation of two notes, *Ullah, ullah, ullah, ullah,* keeping on perpetually. When I passed streets that ran northward, it grew in volume, and houses and buildings seemed to deaden and cut it off again. I stopped, staring towards Kensington Gardens, wondering at this strange, remote wailing. It was as if that mighty desert of houses had found a voice for its fear and solitude.

Drawn by the sound, I wandered on through the silent streets, littered with corpses, until I came out at last upon Regent's Park. And as I emerged from the top of Baker Street, I saw far away over the trees in the clearness of the sunset the hood of the Martian giant from which this howling proceeded. I was not terrified. I came upon him as if it were a matter of course. The tripod did not move. The Martian appeared to be standing and yelling, for no reason that I could discover.

Regent's Canal was choked with the red weed, and it had spread across the grasses and was growing amongst the trees, a spongy mass of dark red vegetation. As I stood watching, the sound of *Ullah, ullah, ullah,* ceased. Cut off. The silence came like a thunderclap.

A terror seized me. The dusky houses about me stood faint and tall and dim; the trees in the park were growing black. Night, the mother of fear and mystery, was coming down.

I fled. In front of me, the road became pitch black as though it was covered in tar, and I saw a contorted shape lying across the pathway. I could not bring myself to go on. I turned down St John's Wood Road and ran headlong from this unendurable stillness towards Kilburn. I hid from the night and the silence, until long after midnight, in a cabmen's shelter in Harrow Road.

Before the dawn my courage returned, and while the stars were still in the sky I headed back towards Regent's Park. I had to know what had happened to the tripod.

As I drew nearer and the light grew, I saw that a multitude of black birds was circling about the hood. At that, my heart gave a bound and I began running along the road.

I felt no fear now, only a wild, trembling exultation as I ran up Primrose Hill towards the motionless monster. Out of the hood hung lank shreds of brown, at which the hungry birds pecked and tore. In a moment I was at the foot of the tripod and scrambled up an earthen rampart. The interior of the redoubt was below me. A mighty space it was, with gigantic machines and strange shelters. And, scattered about it, some in their overturned war machines and some stark and silent laid in a row, were the Martians – dead! Slain, after all man's devices had failed, by the humblest things that God, in His wisdom, has put upon this Earth: the putrefactive and diseased bacteria against which their systems were unprepared.

And now comes the strangest thing in my story. I remember vividly all that I did that day until the time that I stood weeping and praising God upon the summit of Primrose Hill. And then I forget.

Of the next three days that followed I know nothing. I have learned since that, so far from my being the first discoverer of the Martian overthrow, several such wanderers as myself had already discovered it. One man had contrived to telegraph to Paris.

Thence the joyful news had flashed all over the world. Men were making up trains, even as near as Crewe, to descend upon London. The church bells that had ceased a fortnight since suddenly caught the news, until all England was bellringing.

But of all this I have no memory. I drifted, a demented man. I found myself in a house of kindly people, who had found me on the third day wandering, weeping and raving through the streets of St John's Wood. They sheltered me and protected me from myself. Very gently, when my mind was assured again, they confirmed what I already knew: that Leatherhead had been entirely destroyed by the Martians, and every person in it killed.

When I was well enough, I left these kind people. I walked through streets that had lately been so dark and strange and empty. Already they were busy with returning people; in places there were even shops open, and I saw a drinking fountain running water. I remember how mockingly bright the day seemed as I went back on my melancholy pilgrimage to the little house at Woking, how busy the streets and vivid the moving life about me.

The door to my house had been forced; it was opening slowly as I approached, caught by the wind, banged shut again, and again swung wide. The curtains of my study fluttered out of the open window from which I had observed the Martian cylinder descend like a meteor weeks before.

I stumbled into the hall, and the house felt empty. I went up to my study and found, lying on my writing table still, with the selenite paper weight upon it, the sheet of work I had left on the afternoon of the opening of the cylinder.

I went back downstairs. The French window at the back of the house was open. I made a step to it and stood, looking out. And there, amazed and afraid, even as I stood amazed and afraid, was my wife, white and tearless. "I came," she said. "I knew."

I made a step forward and caught her in my arms. We had both been through so much. But even in the bliss of reunion, I could not forget all the death and destruction I had seen. Before us lay the task of rebuilding.

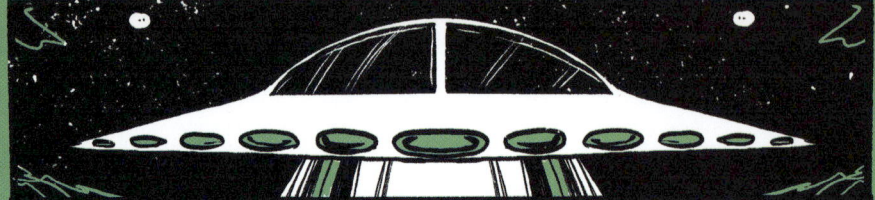

INVADERS FROM OUTER SPACE

We return to *The War of the Worlds* (1898), the earliest and still, I think, the best story of alien invasion. Wells takes from Jules Verne the idea of spacecraft being launched by being fired out of a giant cannon, but he locates that cannon on Mars. According to nineteenth-century beliefs, all the planets had formed by congealing out of space dust and cooling to solidity, with the outermost planets forming first and the innermost planets last. If that was so, Wells reasoned, then Mars – further away from the Sun than Earth – must be much older than Earth. Perhaps its inhabitants were more evolved, further advanced than us in technology. Perhaps Mars was so old that it was dying, its resources exhausted, its waters drying up. In 1877, Italian astronomer Giovanni Schiaparelli, observing Mars through his telescope, thought he saw *canali* on the planet. The word in Italian means 'channels', but his work was mis-translated into English as 'canals', and people began speculating that Martian inhabitants had created these to bring water from the poles to the arid, dying main part of the planet. In this case, Wells wondered, mightn't Mars's inhabitants look to Earth with an envious eye? A young world, still rich in resources. Might they not be tempted to abandon their world and take ours, by force?

In one sense, *The War of the Worlds* was an example of that crowded late nineteenth-century genre: 'future invasion of Britain' tales. The first of this kind of story was George Tomkyns Chesney's *Battle of Dorking* (1871). A huge hit in its day, it imagines a near future in which a small but efficient German army invades Britain and humiliatingly defeats it. The book sold 110,000 copies in two months; it was discussed in the House of Commons and translated into most European languages. Dozens of other authors rushed to write imitations, with England (or America) being invaded by Italians, Russians, the Chinese and others. Wells' brilliant idea was to write a similar tale, replacing human adversaries with alien ones. Wells' Martians are, of course, imperialists. Britain had been accumulating its own Empire throughout the century, conquering many territories around the world because of its superior technological and military sophistication. Wells turns the tables on this situation, asking his readers to imagine how things would be if Britain were invaded by a militaristic and technologically superior force.

Before Wells, inhabitants of other worlds were generally benign, sometimes holy, usually humanoid. With Wells we get the influential and persistent idea that aliens would not only be radically different – his octopoid-tentacled Martians have evolved beyond the use of the regular body – but also malign, hostile, monstrous. They literally suck the blood of the humans they capture, like Bram Stoker's *Dracula* (a novel, coincidentally, published only a year before Wells': the two men had no contact with one another). But where Stoker's vampires represent the dead weight of the aristocratic past, Wells' high-tech and ruthless Martians are a terrifying vision of a possible future.

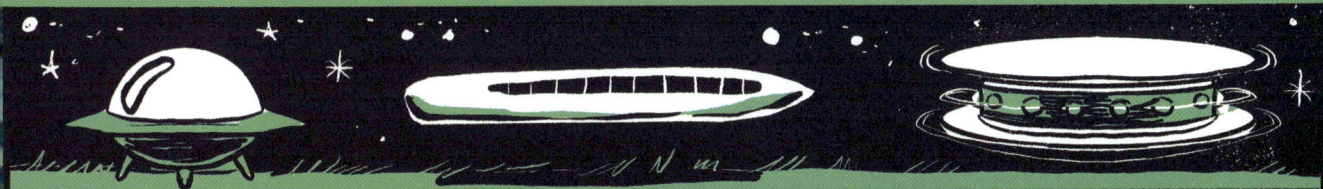

HERLAND

It began this way. There were three of us, classmates and friends: Jeff Margrave and I, Vandyck Jennings, Terry O Nicholson (we used to call him Old Nick, with good reason).

We had known each other years and years, and in spite of our differences we had a good deal in common. All of us were interested in science.

Terry was rich enough to do as he pleased. His great aim was exploration. Terry had all kinds of boats and motorcars, and was one of the best of our airmen.

We never could have done the thing at all without Terry.

Jeff Margrave was born to be a poet or a botanist – or both – but his folks persuaded him to be a doctor instead. He was a good one for his age, but his real interest was in what he loved to call 'the wonders of science'. A finer southern gentleman than Jeff never breathed the air: courteous and chivalrous and brave.

As for me, well: I'm interested in everything. All of it!

We joined an expedition: up among a great river, where maps had to be made, hitherto unknown languages studied, and all manner of strange flora and fauna expected. But this story is not about that expedition. That was only the merest starter for ours.

It began with talk among our guides. I'm quick at languages, picking them up readily. And as we got further and further upstream, in a dark tangle of rivers, lakes, morasses and dense forests, with here and there an unexpected long spur running out from the big mountains beyond, I noticed the guides chattering on about a strange and terrible land in the high distance. "Up yonder," "Over there," "Way up" – was all the direction they could offer. But they all agreed on the main point – that there was this strange country where no men lived – only women and girl children. None of them had ever seen it. It was dangerous, deadly, they said, for any man to go there. But there were tales of long ago, when some brave investigator had seen it.

When I told Terry and Jeff what I had heard, they were immediately fired up: we had to find this place! No good asking the guides to lead us – they were fearful of the place.

There was a biplane, its wings folded up like praying hands, in the cargo of the expedition ship. Terry persuaded the expedition leader to let us unload it, ready it and run it along the beach to get airborne. Then we flew around. Out of that dark green sea of crowding forest, a mountain spur rose steeply, running back on either side to more distant peaks, themselves inaccessible. Flying over this revealed a hidden kingdom: a large lake, fields, meadows and open spaces. There was a grand city, too: nothing like the clusters of huts elsewhere, these were fine stone towers, spacious mansions.

"Looks like a first-rate climate," Terry declared. "It's wonderful what a little height will do for temperature." As we flew over a town, the people heard our engine and ran out of the houses to look up. "Gosh!" cried Terry. "Only women – and children."

"There's a fine landing place right there," Jeff insisted – a wide, flat-topped rock, overlooking the lake and quite out of sight. "They won't find this in a hurry."

So we landed and made our way down the slope. "Come on," Terry urged. Of course it was unwise of us. It was easy to see afterwards that our best plan was to have studied the country fully before we left our plane. But we were young and foolish.

As we took our first steps in this unknown kingdom, we noticed three young women, up in the trees, watching us. They didn't seem scared of us, which confirmed Terry's suspicions. "There must be men here, too. I mean, we saw children, so there must be men. Wait!" he called after the three women as they ran away.

But they were down from the trees now and running. We ran after them through the forest, across a field and into one of the villages. It was rash of us. In the village we were immediately surrounded. Terry tried to brazen it out, but the women were – all of them – agile and strong. Every one of them was tall, long-limbed and rapid: each moved with the perfect grace of the panther, and the direct focus of the hunter.

We were quickly surrounded and, though we struggled and fought, the women overpowered us and bound our hands. Each of us was seized by five women, lifted like helpless children and borne onwards.

We were taken inside a high inner hall and brought before a powerful grey-haired woman who seemed to hold a judicial position. There was some talk among them, and then suddenly there fell upon each of us at once a firm hand holding a wetted cloth before mouth and nose – an odour of swimming sweetness – anaesthesia.

When I awoke I was lying in a perfect bed: long, soft and level, with the finest linen. The room I was in was large, high and wide, with many lofty windows whose closed blinds let through soft, green-lit air.

Terry and Jeff were there too. "Gosh!" said Jeff.

"They haven't hurt us in the least," said Terry. "They could have killed us."

There was no escape from the room, but it soon became apparent that the women did not intend to merely imprison us. Over the following weeks, the women showed us their realm, and taught us their language. I, being quickest with linguistic matters, picked it up easily enough – it was, oddly, a little like Basque, or Welsh – aided by the fact that my teacher, Ellador, was attentive and patient.

The other two found the language harder, though they picked up enough to get by. But they relied on me to translate sometimes – as such times when we were brought before the Council, an assembly of older women.

"This land is for women only," the lead-woman said. "How is it that you – three males – come to be here?"

I explained that we had heard rumours of a 'Herland' and had crossed the mountains to see. I kept to myself exactly how, or where our aeroplane was parked, but I was forgetting that we had been seen, flying through the sky, by many of them, and they had deduced our technology.

"We mean no disrespect," I said. "We are explorers, scientists: we seek only knowledge."

The chairwoman spoke again: "We have been troubled with men before – violent men, savages, who have sought only to harm us. These we have disposed of. But you, it seems, are different. Your flying machine shows that you come from a highly civilised society. Doubtless possessed of much valuable knowledge. You may indeed be dangerous; but we feel we can use you."

The whole story came out, then and later. It seems they had been a society of men and women, who had come to this place and settled it thousands of years before. A volcanic explosion had sealed them in, destroying the only mountain pass out of Herland. Following the disaster, order was lost and an army of rebels sought to take power. There was a bloody uprising in which many men were killed on both sides. After the rebellion had collapsed, the women found themselves in a position to take over the land.

And so they found themselves: only women, in this sealed-away land. It was fertile and temperate, but without men they despaired of producing a new generation to carry on their way of life.

But then one woman – revered as the Queen-Priestess-Mother of Herland – became pregnant. She gave birth to a female child, and four more female children after. The five daughters of this woman also grew up to bear five daughters each. This process rapidly swelled their population – it led to the exaltation of motherhood.

"Parthenogenesis!" Jeff exclaimed. "It is rare in our world, but not unknown. In the usual way of things, a male spermatozoon has half the genetic material needful for life, and a female egg the other half. But it's possible for two eggs to fuse and life to grow. That's what has happened here!"

Over the centuries that followed, the women established a perfect society – a utopia. We were of course fascinated and eager to learn more about this age of women and the history of Herland.

The women of Herland were all in superb health: strong and powerful. Once they invited us to join them in their games, a kind of Herland Olympics: footraces, long-jump, high-jump and wrestling. We men were quite outmatched. Terry was the strongest of us, though I was wiry and had good staying power, and Jeff was a great sprinter and hurdler, but I can tell you those ladies gave us cards and spades. They ran and leaped like deer, by which I mean that they ran not as if it was a performance, but as if it was their natural gait. And their libraries, all the volumes hand-written, contained a wealth of knowledge. Each village had an elected council, and all affairs were decided democratically. Our fate, for instance, was debated throughout the land and voted upon.

Space being limited, Herlanders had chosen not to crowd the place with livestock, instead subsisting on an entirely vegetarian diet. There were some cows and goats who wandered the fields, but these animals were not farmed. Herlanders instead made stews from grains and pulses, and baked the most delicious bread I have ever eaten.

There were no dogs – a fact I noticed early on. When I asked Ellador about this, she was at first puzzled as to what a 'dog' was. But I found in the library a historical account. "Ah, pet wolves, yes," she said. "We have no love for them and so we did away with them all."

"But," I pointed out, "you keep cats!"

"Indeed," she beamed. "We love cats!" I supposed their many feline pets helped keep down vermin and protect the wheatfields from mice and so on.

The truth is, I was falling in love with Ellador. I had never met a woman like her before. Where I came from, women were encouraged to be passive and demure.

Whereas Ellador was direct and energetic, filled with life. I need hardly add that she was beautiful, with long flowing hair and fine-chiselled features, and with eyes that positively shone with brightness.

Terry and Jeff were likewise engaged in what we might call 'courtship': Jeff with Celis, and Terry with Alima.

Jeff, in fact, was sometimes positively tiresome in the way he would dwell reverently and admiringly, and at immense length, on the exalted sentiment and measureless perfection of his Celis. As for Terry – well, Terry made so many false starts and met so many rebuffs that by the time he really settled down to win Alima, he was considerably wiser. Even then, it was not smooth sailing. They broke and quarrelled, over and over; he would rush off to console himself in pursuit of another – but he would drift back to Alima, becoming more and more devoted each time.

By this point, many months into our stay, the women had come to trust us, and we were no longer locked in our dormitory. One day the three of us snuck away and trekked to where we had parked the plane: but the women had been there first. They had sealed the machine away in a bag of tarpaulin-like cloth, far too tough for me to cut with a knife. "We're not getting away in this bird," I said. "Not without the women knowing and approving our leaving."

In truth, I had no wish to go. Ellador and I were in the early days of our romance, and it was marvellous. And there was much to admire in the social organisation of Herland. They were eminently practicable, untethered by any sentimental attachment to 'tradition' or 'religion': if there was something wrong, they reformed it, and were surprised to hear how powerful a force tradition is in our outside societies. "To revere something simply because it is old," Ellador boggled. "It is not logical!"

On another occasion I asked if I might have some milk. The food we ate was delicious, but the only drink was water, and I had seen cows (only cows, never a bull) wandering the fields. "It would be a simple matter to milk one," I said.

Ellador was shocked. "But that milk is for her calf!"

"Well, I suppose so. But I wouldn't want very much."

"You would steal the milk out of the mouth of the calf? This is a terrible thing!"

"Hardly as terrible as..." I began, and then stopped myself. But it was too late: Ellador pressed me on what I was going to say, and I had to confess that, in America, we very often slaughtered the cow, and the calf too - that beefsteak and veal were staple foods. She was horrified. "Living flesh, destroyed in blood and pain, for food? Are there no vegetables in A-mar-rica?"

"Plenty of vegetables," I assured her. "But we like a bit of variety."

She was so shocked she had to walk away. I had to offer many assurances that I liked the vegetarian diet just fine.

Life was so harmoniously balanced, everyone was so wonderful, the time passed by very quickly. But society was difficult to adjust to. Indeed, Jeff, in his adoration for his beloved Celis, began to assume a passive, subordinate role.

There was one thing on which we all agreed: we each loved a different Herlander, and we wished to marry. When we broached this subject, we were met first with non-comprehension, for there is no such thing as marriage in Herland. But we pressed the point, and explained that it was not mere tradition - despised tradition - that moved us. Marriage was a way of signalling our commitment, our desire to be with this one person, and their desire to be with only us.

The Herlanders were persuaded. It did not, in truth, matter overmuch to them, but they were content to allow us our satisfaction. And so we each married. There was a great feast, and much singing and dancing.

In marriage, Ellador remained as forceful, independent and strong-willed as before. I was grateful for the wonderful friendship I had with her and the intense love I felt.

Jeff was entirely devoted to Celis, who soon became pregnant. There was a great deal of excitement amongst the Herlanders at this development, the first - as the council said - 'bi-sexual' pregnancy in two thousand years. There was every chance the baby would be female, of course, but it could also be that it would be a boy.

Things did not pass so smoothly in Terry's marriage, however. I do not doubt his love for Alima, or hers for him, but he was always hot-headed, and he found it hard to adjust to Herlander ways. He expected his wife to take a traditional role, and grew increasingly bad-tempered and frustrated when she did not.

And it was this that brought our time in Herland to an end. Terry, I'm sorry to say, allowed his anger to boil over. When (as he saw it) Alima thwarted him one time too many, he seized her forcefully. The events led to a trial before the Herland high council. Jeff and I attended, of course, but there was little to be said. No allowances could be made for such sacrilegious behaviour.

The sentence was exile. Terry was ordered to return to his homeland. "We will release your flying machine from its container so you may pilot it away, and you must never return."

Terry was broken by this news, for he really loved Alima and had flourished in Herland. But there was nothing for it.

I realised that I must accompany Terry home in the biplane. Operating it was a two-man job, and Terry was so broken-spirited that I didn't want him going out alone. When I explained this to Ellador she insisted she could not let me leave without her. We went back to the council and pled our case.

"I give you my word," I said, "that I shall not reveal the location of this land to anyone outside – and Terry likewise. Our word is our bond. You will not be bothered from outside on our account."

"You may go," said the presiding judge. "And may, in time, return. But the other man is banished forever. And he must swear. If you will not swear then you must remain here, in prison."

I talked Terry round. Eventually he did swear, and the three of us tramped, accompanied by a dozen Herlanders, to the site where the biplane was. Not Jeff: he chose to stay behind and live in Herland with Celis and their soon-to-be child. I tried to ready Ellador for the kind of world she would find outside her utopia. She was excited. "You have awakened within me," she said, "a spirit like unto yours – you have made me an explorer!"

And so we left Herland.

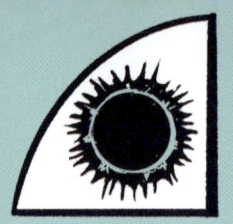

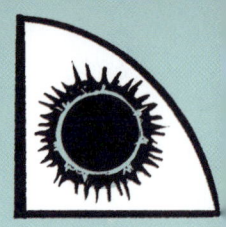

WRITING THE FUTURE

An important part of science fiction is imagining how society might be different: worse – a style of writing we call dystopia – or better. Imagining better worlds comes first, which is in itself a testimony to the fundamental optimism of human creativity. Thomas More (Sir Thomas More, if you have regard for his standing in the British aristocracy, Saint Thomas More if you think his canonisation by the Catholic church takes precedence: Debrett's suggests the first outranks the second) wrote the first utopian novel in 1516. He called his imaginary land 'utopia' as a kind of pun: -*topos* is the Greek for 'place' or 'land', and *u*- means 'not', but also (the Greek *eu*-) 'good'. So, More's *nowhereland* is also his *goodplaceland*, a made-up island upon which society is much better organised and the people are much happier than in the real world.

The success of *Utopia* was immense. From the sixteenth to the nineteenth century, hundreds and hundreds of 'utopian' books were published, and utopia continued to be a major strand of speculative writing into the twentieth century. The opposite term, 'dystopia' (*dys*-, 'bad' replacing the *eu*- 'good') is not coined for another 350 years – in 1868, by John Stuart Mill, in a speech in the House of Commons denouncing the government's Irish land policy. The first dystopian novel, H G Wells' *When The Sleeper Wakes*, was published in 1899, and spawned many imitators.

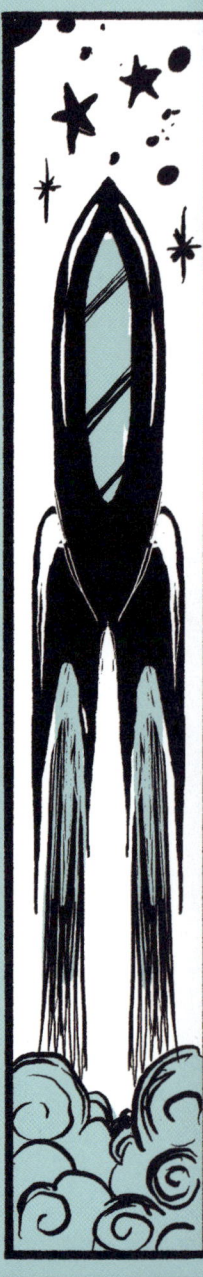

Wells more-or-less single-handedly invented dystopian literature, together with many of its fixtures and fittings. But though dystopian novels are in fashion at the moment – think of Margaret Atwood's *The Handmaid's Tale* (1985), Suzanne Collins' *Hunger Games* books (2008–10), Malorie Blackman's *Noughts and Crosses* (2008) and many others – utopia is still alive, and still a vital part of science fiction: *Star Trek: Federation* or Iain M Banks' *Culture* series to mention two.

American writer Charlotte Perkins Gilman (1860–1935) was an early feminist, and her version of utopia is woman-only – as if to say that what is wrong with society in general is men. Just as More's utopia is an island, and so separated from the rest of the world, so Gilman locks her all-female society away behind impenetrable mountains. But having subsisted happily for thousands of years, their world is about to be invaded by the twentieth century, and the power of aeroplanes to vault mountain walls.

Gilman believed masculine aggressiveness and female maternal impulses were socially conditioned and artificialities, no longer needed for survival in the modern age. 'There is no female mind,' she said in 1898. 'The brain is not an organ of sex. Might as well speak of a female liver.' She argued that there should be no difference in the clothes worn by little girls and boys, or how they play. For her, tomboys were the perfect humans, enjoying and using their bodies freely and healthily. Her 'feminist' utopia is actually a post-gender utopia, and that makes it especially relevant for the twenty-first century.

BUCK ROGERS: ARMAGEDDON 2419 AD

I begin with this declaration: I, Anthony Rogers, known to my friends as 'Buck', am, so far as I know, the only man alive whose normal span of eighty-one years of life has been spread over a period of 573 years. To be precise, I lived the first twenty-nine years of my life between 1898 and 1927, and the latter fifty-two years since 2419. The gap between these two, a period of nearly five hundred years, I spent in a state of suspended animation, free from the ravages of catabolic processes, and without any apparent effect on my physical or mental faculties.

When I began my long sleep, man had only just begun his conquest of the air, in rickety aeroplanes driven by internal combustion motors. Radio and television were but new technologies, and harnessing the power of the atom was but a dream.

I awoke 500 years later to find the America I knew a wreck – Americans a hunted race in their own land, hiding in the dense forests that covered the shattered and levelled ruins of their once magnificent cities.

A new empire had arisen, based on an alliance of European and Asian peoples, the so-called 'Pan-Eurasian' civilization. World domination was in the hands of these Pans, and the centre of world power lay in that great stretch of land from Spain to China.

America remained, in this new age, one of the few peoples unsubdued – not, it must be admitted, because the Pan were incapable of it, but because in the eyes of the Pan airlords who ruled North America as titular tributaries of the Most Magnificent Emperor, they were not worth the trouble. They needed not the forests in which the Americans lived, nor the resources of the vast territories these forests covered. With the perfection to which they had reduced the synthetic production of necessities and luxuries, their remarkable development of scientific processes and mechanical accomplishment of work, they had no economic need for the forests, and no economic desire for the enslaved labour of an unruly race. They had all they needed for their magnificently luxurious scheme of civilization, within the walls of the fifteen cities of sparkling glass they had flung skywards on the sites of ancient American centres, into the bowels of the Earth underneath them.

How did I come to be here? In 1927 I ran a company called the American Radioactive Gas Corporation. I had been hired to investigate reports of strange phenomena observed in an abandoned coal mine near the Wyoming Valley, Pennsylvania. I descended, with two assistants and all our equipment, to explore the mine. Inside we soon found a quantity of hydrovanadate of uranium, and other metals and radium compounds.

But disaster struck. In the lower levels, the radioactivity had degraded the integrity of the miners' struts. The tunnel we were in shuddered and collapsed. I was able to leap ahead into a cave, but my companions were, alas, crushed and killed instantly. I was trapped. Return was impossible. With my electric torch I explored the cave to its end, but could find no other way out. The air became increasingly difficult to breathe, from the rapid accumulation of the radioactive gas. I lost consciousness.

When I awoke, there was a refreshing circulation of cool air in the shaft. I assumed I had been unconscious no more than a few hours, although in fact the radioactive gas had kept me in a state of suspended animation through five centuries, and more.

My awakening, I realised later, was due to seismic shifting of the rock-strata above me, which reopened the shaft and cleared the atmosphere. This must have been the case, for I was able to struggle back up the shaft over a pile of debris and stagger up the long incline to the mouth of the mine, where an entirely different world, overgrown with a vast forest and no visible sign of human habitation, met my eyes.

I wandered the unfamiliar forest like a lost soul. Soon enough, hunger compelled me to action. I fashioned a trap and made myself a club, and so caught food, roasting it over a fire I kindled by hand. It dawned on me that I had been in my suspended animation for a very long time.

I had been wandering along aimlessly, musing over my strange fate, when I saw a figure emerging from the dense growth across the glade. It seemed to be a lad of fifteen or sixteen, and his attention was tensely on the heavy growth of trees from which he had just emerged. He was wearing tight-fitting garments entirely of green, and a helmet of the same colour, and a broad belt.

There was a sudden flash and detonation, like a hand grenade, not far to our left. He staggered and continued retreating, aiming his pistol at the trees. There was neither flash nor detonation from the muzzle of the weapon itself, but wherever he pointed there was a terrific explosion.

The boy leaped, sailing through the air in such a jump as I had never in my life seen before. That leap must have carried him a full fifty feet. His 'knapsack' was evidently some manner of elevating device.

When he alighted, his foot caught on a projecting root and he fell hard. I rushed to him, saw the blood trickling from beneath his helmet, and saw that he was stunned. Taking up his weapon, I found it not unlike the automatic pistol to which I was accustomed. As his pursuers – three of them – broke from the cover of the trees, I raised the gun and fired. They leaped into the air and floated much as the boy had done. My aim was bad, for there was no kick in the gun, so I missed the group of pursuers and hit a tree – but though the weapon was soundless, its destructive power was immense. The trees exploded, hurling fragments in every direction and felling the pursuers entirely. They tumbled to the ground.

Now I had time to give some attention to my companion. She was, I found, a girl, and not a boy. She was very slender and very pretty. There was a stream not far away, from which I brought water and bathed her face and wound. Apparently the mystery of these long leaps, the monkey-like ability to jump such distances, lay in the belt: some manner of anti-gravity device.

When the girl came to, she regarded me as curiously as I did her, and promptly began to quiz me. Her accent and intonation puzzled me a lot, but nevertheless we were able to understand each other fairly well, except for certain words and phrases. I explained what had happened while she lay unconscious, and she thanked me simply for saving her life.

"What gang do you belong to?" (She pronounced it gan, with only a suspicion of a nasal sound.)

I laughed. "I'm not a gangster," I said. But she evidently did not understand this word.

"Does everybody belong to a gang nowadays?" I asked.

"Naturally," she said, frowning. "If you don't belong to a gang, where and how do you live? Why have you not found and joined a gang? How do you eat? Where do you get your clothing?"

"I've been eating wild game for the past two weeks," I explained, "and this clothing I— er—' I saw that I would have to explain that I was many hundred years old. I told my story as well as I could, piecing it together with my assumptions as to what had happened. She listened patiently; incredulously at first, but with more confidence as I went on.

"My name is Wilma Deering," she said. "I was on patrol when I was attacked by an enemy gang, the Bad Bloods. They are Americans, but they have betrayed the nation and allied themselves with the Pans.'

And so I first heard of the overlordship of the Pans.

Wilma took me back to her camp to meet the bosses of her gang. On the way, she filled me in on what had passed since I fell into my radioactive coma. It seems a war had broken out between Europe and Asia in the year 2019, and that, rather than one side winning or the other, it had been resolved with a union of the two landmasses. This 'Pan' empire had then spread out to conquer the world, by virtue of their immensely powerful aeroplane fleets. The 'Airlords of Pan' ruled North America as they ruled everywhere else: a province of the world empire. Not content with conquering the globe, the Pan empire had fashioned rocket-craft that could pass through the vacuum of space, and had landed on the Moon, and fought the Tiger Men of Mars.

The Airlords swept in over the Pacific and Atlantic coasts, annihilating American aircraft, armies and cities with their terrific disintegrator rays, projected from a machine not unlike a searchlight in appearance: a terribly destructive beam. Under its influence, material substance melted into nothingness; i.e., into electronic vibrations. It destroyed all known substances, from air to the densest metals and stone.

Against such military and technological superiority, resistance seemed futile. Yet the Americans I met, largely ignored by the Pan authorities and left to fend for themselves in the forests and mountains, were a resilient and determined bunch. Living in cooperative gangs and hiding in the woodland, they had been secretly rebuilding their civilization for hundreds of years, and developing new technologies. One of these I had already seen: inertron, an anti-gravitational substance with 'reverse weight', which enabled the 'jumpers' by which she had leaped so impressively.

Wilma brought me to Big Boss Hart, head of her gang. "Amazing to think you come to us out of the deep past," he said. "But maybe we can learn some things from you. You fought in the First World War?"

"I did."

"We have very little left in the way of records of the details of that war. We forgot many things during the Pan terror and, well, I think you might have a lot of ideas worth thinking over for our raid masters. By the way, now that you're here and can't go back to your own century, what do you want to do? You're welcome to become one of us."

"I'd like to fight for America against this Pan tyranny," I said.

"Excellent! I'm going to send you over to Bill Hearn. He's Camp Boss of number thirty-four. There's a vacancy in his camp."

Bill, like all the others, was clad in green. He was a big man – that is, he was about my own height (five feet and eleven inches) which was considerably above the average now, for the race had lost something in stature.

I got the chance to familiarise myself with the community life. It was not easy. There were so many marvels to absorb. I never ceased to wonder at the strange combination of the provincial social life and feverish industrial activity. In my experience, industrial development meant crowded cities, paved streets, tower-blocks and noise. Here, however, was rural simplicity, with isolated families and groups living in the heart of the forest and a total absence of crowds. There was no means of conveyance other than the belts called jumpers, and an occasional rocket ship, used only for longer journeys, plus underground plants or factories that supplied all needs, and were more like laboratories than engine rooms.

Gang members stayed in contact with one another by means of ultronic broadcast. Ultron is used not only for communications, but as a way of detecting the incoming Pan airships – and for generating a shield against their disintegrator rays, although this is not a perfect defence.

All able-bodied men and women alternated in two-week periods between military and industrial service, except those who were needed for household work. Since working conditions in the plants and offices were ideal, and everybody thus had plenty of healthy outdoor activity in addition, the population was sturdy and active. Laziness was regarded as nearly the greatest of social offences. Hard work and general merit were variously rewarded with extra privileges, advancement to positions of authority, and with various items of personal equipment for convenience and luxury. In leisure moments, I got great enjoyment from sitting outside the dwelling in which I was quartered with Bill Hearn and ten other men, watching the occasional passers-by as, with leisurely but swift movements, they swung up and down the forest trail, rising from the ground in long, almost horizontal leaps, swinging from one convenient branch overhead to another before sliding back to the ground further on. Such things as automobiles and railroad trains (the memory of them not more than a month old in my mind) seemed inexpressibly silly and futile compared with such convenience as these belts or jumpers offered.

There was a girl in Wilma's camp named Gerdi Mann, with whom Bill Hearn was desperately in love, and the four of us used to go around a lot together. Gerdi was a distinct type. While Wilma had the usual dark brown hair and hazel eyes that marked nearly every member of the community, Gerdi had red hair, blue eyes and very fair skin. She has been dead many years now, but I remember her vividly.

One day we were startled by an alarm rocket that burst high in the air, spreading a pall of red smoke.

"A Pan raid!" Bill exclaimed. "The first in seven years!"

"They're sweeping the countryside with their dis beams," said Wilma in some agitation.

"We had better get under cover," Gerdi said nervously.

The standard orders covering air raids were that the population was to scatter individually. Experience of generations had proved that if this were done, and everybody remained hidden beneath the tree screens, the Pans would have to sweep mile after mile of territory, foot by foot, to catch more than a small percentage of the community. Gerdi, however, refused to leave Bill, and Wilma developed an equal obstinacy against quitting my side. I was inexperienced at this sort of thing, she explained.

We all moved beneath the trees and kept an eye on the approaching Pan craft. In the distance, it looked like a phantom dirigible airship, in its coat of low-visibility paint, a bare spectre. "Seven thousand feet up," Wilma whispered, crouching close to me.

The ship was operating two disintegrator rays. Whenever they flashed downwards, with blinding brilliancy, forest, rocks and ground melted instantaneously into nothing. The work of destruction began systematically. Back and forth travelled the destroying rays, ploughing parallel furrows from hillside to hillside.

"This is awful," Wilma moaned. "How could they know the location so exactly, Buck?"

We knew that many of our companions must have been whisked into absolute non-existence before our eyes in these few moments.

"How far will this gun shoot, Wilma?" I demanded, drawing my pistol.

"Why? You couldn't penetrate the shell of that ship with rocket force, even if you could reach it."

But I had an idea I wanted to try, a hunch. The ship flew by means of a 'repeller' ray where three powerful beams directed at the ground kept it aloft. I fired my rocket-pistol not at the armoured bulk of the ship, but into this ray. As soon as the rocket passed into this force, it exploded, with enough force to disable the ray's generator. The whole craft came tumbling out of the sky to crash and burn upon the ground. The sound of its detonation reverberated from the hills – the momentum of eighteen or twenty thousand tons, in a sheer drop of seven thousand feet.

Wilma cheered, and I could hear other cries of delight from throughout the woodland. But the consequences were severe. "We must scatter," Wilma exclaimed. "In half an hour there'll be an entire Pan fleet here from New York. They'll receive this news instantly on their recordographs and location finders. They'll blast the whole valley and the country for miles beyond. Come, Buck! We've got to jump. Oh, I'm so proud of you!"

Over the ridge we went, in long leaps towards the east, the country of the Delawares.

We were received by the gangs in Delaware as heroes. I showed people how I had been able to use my rocket-pistol to bring down the Pan craft.

We knew the Pan fleet was coming, and from which direction, so I organised our defences. Hundreds of snipers, with rocket-pistols and rocket-rifles, hidden through the trees.

We heard the approach of the Pan craft before we saw them. But on they came, sweeping the ground beneath with their destructo-rays.

"On the count of three," I called, "shoot up those repeller rays – all of them – and for God's sake, don't miss!"

The shots went up, and though many missed, enough hit their target to damage the huge ships. One careened off to the side, and a moment later another vast hulk crashed to Earth. There was a period of explosions and crashes. When I next looked out, the only Pan craft in the sky were two smaller scout-ships away to the south, which were hanging perpendicularly and sagging slowly down. Somebody hit the other repeller ray of one of the two remaining ships, and it fell out of sight beyond a hilltop. The other, further away, drifted down diagonally, its disintegrator ray playing viciously over the ground below it.

I shouted with exultation and relief. But the fighting wasn't over. A number of Pan air-soldiers had leaped from the plummeting craft, and many had anti-gravity jumpers that meant they were able to reach the ground unharmed.

I led a squad to mop up these remnants. We burst through the trees and met a knot of Pan troops in a clearing. For an instant they stood frozen with horror. They were not armed with rocket-pistols – too dangerous to have such weapons loose aboard the sky-ships – and had only knives. We made short work of them. One hurled his knife at me and it grazed my cheek. The rest made a break for the trees. We fired point-blank with our handguns, pressing the button as fast as we could and aiming at their feet to make sure the explosive rockets would make contact and do their work. The detonations of my rockets were deafening. The spot on which the Pans stood flashed into a blinding glare. Then there was nothing there.

There was a great deal of celebration at this victory. And the day after it, Wilma and I got married, and I was officially inducted into her gang.

"I think I know how the Pan were able to target our hidden base so well," I told her. "It must be the Bad Blood gang – they have been spying on us and informing the Pans of what they see."

The treason would continue, and the Pans would continue to attack if we didn't deal with the Bad Bloods. I organised a posse and led it into their territory, but found it deserted.

"They knew we would come for them," said Wilma. "See where they have fled – they've taken themselves to the Pan city of New York."

"Well, then: New York is where we must go."

The assault on such an important Pan city was no small matter. It required the coordination of a dozen gangs, training and practice with arms, and detailed plans. It turned out that, brave though these New Americans were, only I possessed the experience of prolonged, systematic combat. I was made War Boss and given all the authority of a general.

The centrepiece of my planned assault was one of the Pan ships. Many had been completely destroyed, but one of the scout ships was not too badly damaged, and we were able to repair it. Learning how to operate its repeller ray took practice, and once it was up in the air, we didn't know how to land it safely. But that didn't matter. I didn't plan on landing it. We would stuff it with explosives and fly it into the Pan central communication tower, in the heart of New York, disabling their coordination. We, meanwhile, would abandon her in flight and sink to the ground with our anti-gravbelts.

"No one has attempted anything this bold," Wilma told me.

I took her in my arms and kissed her. "That is why it is going to work," I told her.

We boarded our ship before dawn and steered it into the sky. By the time the Sun began to rise, we were approaching New York.

Setting the ultron-wire reel to guide it to its final destination, we climbed through the ship's cargo doors and began to glide down gently, leaving the ship behind.

There was nothing to see as we sank through a layer of cloud, but when we emerged, there came under my gaze, about a mile below, one of the most beautiful sights I have ever seen: the soft, yet brilliant, radiance of the great Pan city of New York. Every foot of its structural members seemed to glow with a wonderful incandescence, tower piled up on tower, and all built on the vast base-mass of the city which, so I had been told, sheered upwards from the surface of the rivers to a height of 728 levels. The city, I noticed with some surprise, did not cover anything like the same area as the New York of the twentieth century. It occupied, as a matter of fact, only the lower half of Manhattan Island.

We landed in what had once been Central Park, and immediately spread out.

The first the Pan knew of our assault was when the now-empty craft crashed into their communication structure in a shower of flame and destruction. Then our troops moved quickly through the city, leaping from city block to city block.

Men set up rocket-rifles on tripods and made good use of them, sending small projectiles arching into the air to fall precisely five miles ahead and explode with the force of eight-inch shells, such as we used in the First World War.

The Pan soldiers were easy to defeat. Harder were the Bad Blood gang members, who knew they were fighting for their very lives. The Pan seemed too shocked by the mere fact of our attack to be able to fight back.

Some Pan airships moved through the sky overhead, but they could not use their destructor rays for fear of hitting their own, and when I launched a rocket-bullet that exploded one of them, they flew off, over the Atlantic and away.

In less than an hour the battle was over, and New York was ours.

The effectiveness of our barrage tactics established a confidence in our ability to overcome the Pans. As I pointed out to Wilma, "It has been my belief all along that the American explosive rocket is a far more efficient weapon than the disintegrator ray of the Pans, once we can train all our gangs to use it systematically and in a coordinated fashion. The dis ray inevitably reveals its source of emanation. The rocket gun does not. The dis ray can reach its target only in a straight line. The rocket may be made to travel in an arc, over intervening obstacles, to an unseen target."

I embraced Wilma. "The Finger of Doom points squarely at the Pans today," I said. "And unless you and I are killed in the struggle, we shall live to see America drive them entirely from this land."

FROM PAGE TO SCREEN

In the first half of the twentieth century, science fiction burgeoned. It grew in popularity and reach, and nowhere was this florescence more notable than in the pulps. The 'pulps' are so-called from the quality of the paper upon which were printed a great many magazines in the 1920s, '30s and '40s. Paper made from recycled pulped woodchip was relatively inexpensive, and publishers looking to cut costs and maximise profits produced a great many magazines printed upon this material. The first pulp was called *Argosy* (originally appearing in 1882, it lasted until 1972), printing various kinds of short stories and articles. Genre-specific pulps soon appeared, specialising in crime, or adventure, or romance. In April 1926, the first science fiction pulp emerged: *Amazing Stories*, edited by Hugo Gernsback. More soon followed, and by the 1930s there were dozens of science fiction pulps: exciting, propulsive, often outlandish narratives of space adventure, written in haste and consumed in large quantities. The energy and variety of pulp is an important element in science fiction.

As an example of the kind of thing that filled the many pulp science fiction magazines in the 1920s and 1930s, I've included the very first 'Buck Rogers' story. After a number of prose adventures and a comic-strip, Buck Rogers was adapted for the cinema. *Buck Rogers in the 25th Century: An Interplanetary Battle with the*

Tiger Men of Mars premiered at the 1933 Chicago World's Fair, and a popular movie serial followed later in the 1930s, starring former Olympic gold-medal swimmer Larry 'Buster' Crabbe as Buck.

The series was resurrected on TV from 1979–1981 – *Buck Rogers in the 25th Century* – and a new feature film adaptation is in the offing. The kinetic, energetic, sometimes gnashing and breathless style of pulp is well illustrated in the first Buck Rogers adventure, written originally by Philip Francis Nowlan. In one respect, this adaptation has been changed. In the original, the villains were Chinese, and in his original characterisation Nowlan lays on racist orientalism and hostility with a trowel. In this version of his story, the enemy has been replaced by the 'Pan', a Pan-Eurasian alliance bent on global domination. Otherwise, though, the story is presented pretty much as it was first published, across several issues of Gernsback's *Amazing Stories*, published between 1928 and 1929.

The success of Buck Rogers inspired Alex Raymond to create a cartoon strip in which a similar character, Flash Gordon, had similar kinds of space adventures. The comic was very successful, and Universal adapted it into a thirteen-episode film serial, starring Buster Crabbe: *Flash Gordon* (1936). Two more serials followed. George Lucas, who grew up watching these films when they were repeated on television in the 1950s, has spoken of how much they influenced *Star Wars* (1977), the most successful science fiction movie of all time. Heroes and villains, exciting adventure and space battles, bug-eyed monsters and bizarre aliens, derring-do and sense-of-wonder. Pulp lives on.

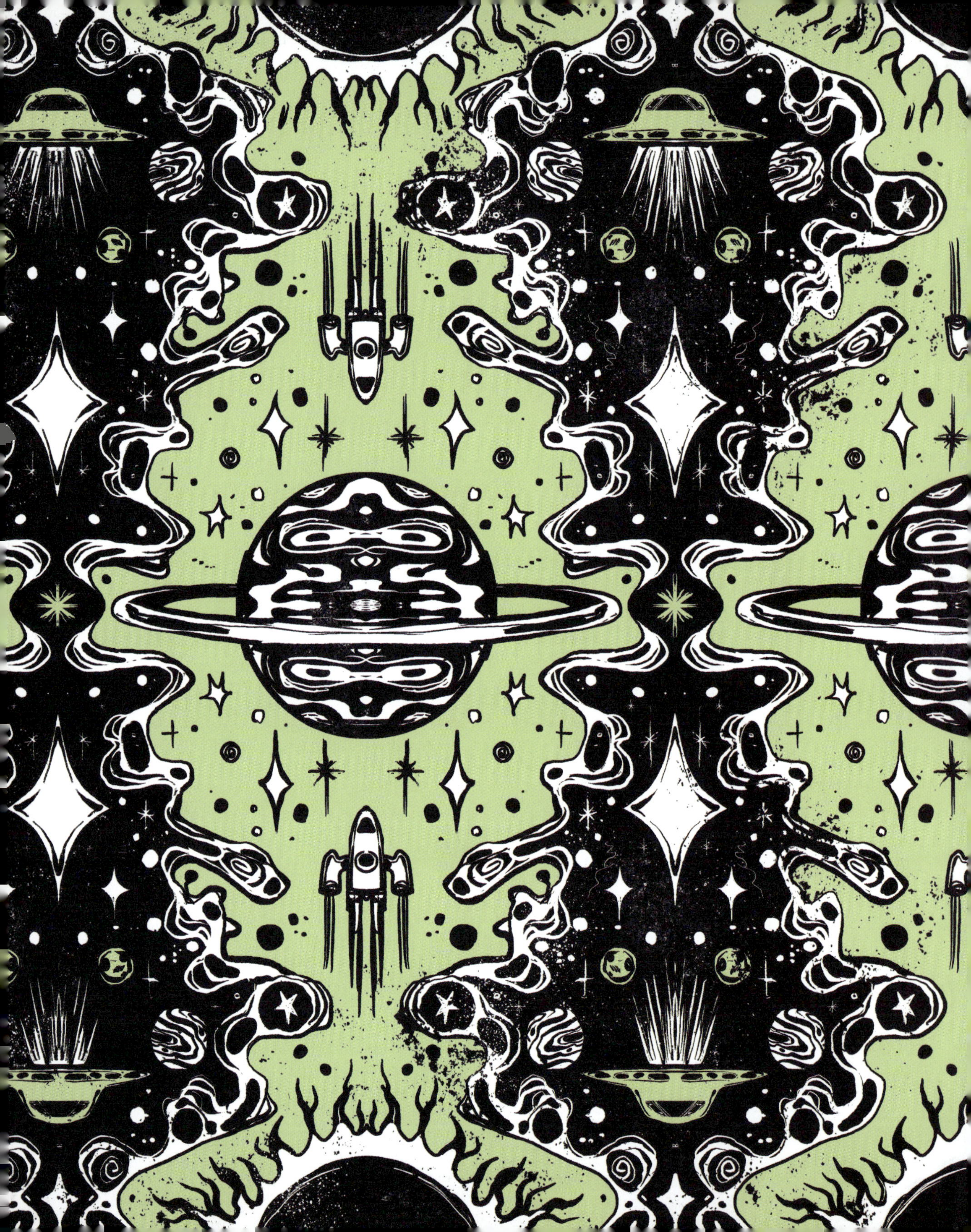